Brendon: Encouraged to Praise

The Barnabas Chronicles
Book 8

By

Ronna M. Bacon

Nahum 1:7
The Lord is good,
A stronghold in the day of trouble;
And He knows those who trust in Him.
NKJV

Psalm 34
1. I will bless the Lord at all times;
His praise shall continually be in my mouth.
2. My soul shall make its boast in the Lord;
The humble shall hear of it and be glad.
3. Oh, magnify the Lord with me,
And let us exalt His name together.
4. I sought the Lord, and He heard me,
And delivered me from all my fears.
NKJV

Table of Contents

Hearing the bell signaling someone had entered the front of the cabinetry shop where he worked, Brendon Conroy sighed, staring down at the dark-stained latex gloves he was wearing and then at the end table he had almost finished staining. A quick decision had him returning to the staining. It just can't wait, he thought. If I leave it, then I have to start all over with a new table, and that I just can't do. Lord, why now? I'm on my own, Lawrence is away doing deliveries. He finally stripped off the gloves, tossing them into a waste receptacle on his way to the front, his mind still on the work he needed to accomplish that day. Not a lot, he thought, given that it was a long holiday weekend coming up and he was looking forward to that. The cabinetry shop had become quite busy, and Lawrence was happy, but Brendon just wanted a break. He hadn't had time off in a close to a year, he thought, other than when he had taken time to work on finding the culprits in the adventures his friends at the Barnabas Foundation seemed determined to have.

Running a hand through his jet-black hair, Brendon paused just inside the workroom, peering through the doorway, not seeing anyone in the showroom, but he knew he had heard the doorbell. He shook his head before he walked out onto the floor, searching about the model furniture that Lawrence had set up in it. He frowned as he studied the short, heavyset man who was standing at the window, staring out, appearing to be just a customer, but something about him rang alarms bells in Brendon's mind. He had seen too many of his friends go through danger not to be concerned. Lord, I have no idea what I am about to face, but You do. Please, protect me.

"Can I help you?" Brendon paused in the middle of the room, his eyes scanning quickly for anything that was out of the ordinary. He faintly heard the buzzer as the back door opened and frowned some more. That couldn't be Lawrence, he thought. He had indicated that he would not be back today, at least not until dark.

The man turned slowly, a sneer covering his face, as he looked Brendon up and down. "I'm looking for a young lady. She was seen entering these premises." The man's hand flicked in disdain at the furniture. "Though why she would do that is beyond me."

Brendon shrugged, his dark gray eyes watchful. "Haven't seen or heard anyone today. I've been too busy. If that's all you want, there's the door." His head nodded that way as he squinted at his watch. "I need to lock up. It's closing time."

"No, it's not." The man pranced forward, his shiny dress shoes seeming too small for his feet. "It's not four o'clock yet."

"But you see, I can close up early. I'm in charge this afternoon, and I say the business is closed." Brendon paced over to the door, anger briefly flaring in him, as he yanked open the door and held out a hand for the man to leave. "I have no idea who you are, or who you are looking for, but I do know that you're not looking for any furniture. So I would suggest you leave and leave now."

"I'll have your job, young man." The man's anger became palpable.

Brendon suddenly grinned. "Go for it. I doubt that will work." He barely let the man get through the door before he had slammed the door, shoved home the locks, turned the open sign to closed, and then pulled down the blind on the door. He moved to one side where he could see the man, who stood in the parking lot, staring around before he walked around the building. He stood once more in the parking lot before he approached the door, shaking it and then hammering at it, demanding that it be opened for him. Brendon grinned to himself. This time, it wouldn't work. He had a good idea of who this was, a new import to an accounting firm in town, and one who had alienated everyone that he had been in contact with.

Brendon moved back through the showroom, flicking off the lights before he paused at the doorway to the workroom, feeling someone was there, but not seeing anyone. He shrugged, putting it off to being tired and needing to get away. His thoughts turned to his plans for the next week, a week that he had booked off, desperately needing a break. He had no real plans, he decided, but just knew he wanted to get away.

Cleaning up from his staining and setting everything back into its place, Brendon walked back through the showroom, ensuring all the windows were closed and locked, and everything there was ready for the weekend. He ducked his head to stare out the window, a smile creeping across his face as he watched his unruly guest pacing the parking lot, every so often glaring at the building. He turned, heading for the office, and setting it to rights for the weekend, before he paused, a frown crossing his face. No, he thought, there can't be anyone here but I did hear the back door buzzer. He began a systemic search, finally stopping near a large table and waiting before he ducked, a hand coming out to grasp the arm of the person hiding under it, pulling them out and to their feet.

Shock covered his face as he realized that the young man that he thought he was pulling out was really a young lady, around his age. His hand dropped from her wrist before he reached for her arm, leading her to a chair and then shoving her down, crouching down near her.

He watched carefully as she refused to look up before he sighed, rising to his feet and heading for the kitchen, to return with a bottle of water, finding the young woman heading for the back door. His long legs covered the distance quickly and a hand on her arm had her stopping, a whimper coming from her. He frowned once more at that and then spun her to face him, a gasp that he couldn't control wrenched from him at the bruising he could see on her face.

"Who did this to you?" His demands were met with silence. "I asked you, who did this to you?"

She shook in fear before she glanced up at him. "He did." Her voice was barely audible.

"Who did?" Brendon was at a loss to know who she meant.

"He did. The man that you were talking to." She wrapped her arms around herself, her face white with fatigue and pain and fear, the dark bruising, some of it turning yellow and green, showing ghastly against it.

"He did? When?" Brendon shook his head. "What am I do to with you? I can't let you out there. He's still waiting." He watched her shivering and sighed once more, pacing to the office and returning with his jean jacket, wrapping it around her, feeling her flinch at his light touch.

She pulled away from him, intent on finding the door and disappearing. Only, Brendon wouldn't let her. He reached past her, a hand flat on the door, holding it closed even as she tugged at the handle.

"Please? Let me go! I need to disappear. If you help me, he'll hurt you." Tears of fear and fatigue trickled down her cheeks and she swiped at them angrily.

Brendon's heart broke for her. *Lord? Is this why I didn't take today off as I had planned? I needed to be here for this lady, whoever she is. And I feel myself being drawn into an adventure, just like my seven friends have already had. I hadn't planned on that, but You did. You planned this, didn't you, Lord? And now that I've met this lady, even without knowing her name, I just cannot walk away from her.*

His hand slipped to her wrist and grasped it lightly, not letting her pull it away from him. He reached into his pocket for his keys, quickly opening the door and pulling her through before the door closed behind him, the security system set. He pointed to his truck parked nearby.

"That's my vehicle. In you go. Here, crouch down for a moment until we're out of here and then you can sit upright." He watched as she did that very thing before he closed the door and headed around the truck to climb up and behind the wheel, pulling away and out of the back of the lot, noting that the man had appeared, hands waving at him to stop. He grinned. *Not this time, buddy. Not with this lady on board. I'm taking her to Anna and Doc. They'll help with her.* He had referred to an older couple in the Barnabas

Foundation building, Doc an emergency room physician, and his wife, Anna, who mothered all fourteen of the men and now the wives of some of the men.

Brendon pulled to the side of the road, shoving the transmission into park before he turned to the young lady with him. By this time, she had sat up on the seat, the seatbelt tight around her, and her hands clutching at his jacket, trying to get warm. She had no idea who he was or where he was taking her, but she felt safe for the first time in months. He will want an explanation, and I don't know that I can give him one, at least one that will make sense.

Brendon studied her in the fading daylight before he grinned.

"I'm Brendon Conroy. I am happy to meet you. And you would be?"

She shook for a moment, terror getting the better of her before his even baritone voice soothed her. She fingered her shoulder-length deep red hair before her dark brown eyes looked at him.

"Imly. Imly Dickerson."

"Emily? I am pleased to meet you." He watched as she shook her head. "What did I say?"

"It's not Emily. It's Imly - spelled i-m-l-y. A hangover from my mother's Irish heritage." Her head went back and her eyes closed for a moment, despair briefly flickering across her face. "I need to leave, Brendon. Being here with you puts you in danger. He won't stop until he finds me."

"And just what is it that he wants from you?" Brendon could feel the anger burning in him again, and had to pray hard to have it tamped down.

Imly stared at him. "You don't know him?"

"I know of him. I've seen him around town. No one likes him or wants anything to do with him." He stared at her, determined to get to the root of the issue. "But why is he after you?"

"He wants something from me. Something that isn't mine to give." Imly blinked rapidly. "My parents are not rich, not in money, but in heritage and ancestry, they are. He's not. He wants from my parents' documents that would allow him to claim a heritage to a clan that isn't his to have. It can only go to the oldest in the family. And that is me when I turn 28, which will be shortly." She turned to face Brendon. "He is determined to get it one way or another, even if he has to marry me. That's why he beat me. I refused. I can't stand him. He is evil personified."

"Then, we will defeat him. That I can promise you. What else does he want?" Brendon waited before he spoke again. "There has to be something more."

"There is. There are rumours that the clan here in Ontario that Mom and Dad are part of has a hidden trove of jewels, gold, and documents that would indict leadership in this town in crimes. He's part of it, I think." Imly looked up, a scream rising from her throat, as a heavy object slammed against the window beside her, fracturing the glass into tiny pieces, but that didn't totally shatter the window.

Brendon took one look at the window and at Imly and then, transmission in drive, floored his accelerator and took off, leaving the man standing behind him, shaking a fist and waving the tire iron he held in the other hand.

"Is he for real?" He sped away from town, driving as fast as he felt he should, heading for the

Barnabas Foundation building and safety. "I'm taking you to the building that I live in. There's an older couple there who will take care of you. Doc can assess your bruises, and don't refuse. We need to document these for the police. We also have a friend, a detective, who would come and talk to you."

Imly merely nodded, not sure of anything anymore. It was the first time in five or six months, she thought, that she felt safe and protected. Lord, are You still there? It seems You Haven't been, but You must be, to lead me to this man, who is so willing to help where others wouldn't.

Chapter 2

Finishing his examination or as much of it as he could, Doc Andrews finally moved from their spare room, leaving Anna with Imly, who was trying hard to convince the older woman that she just could not stay. She had brought danger with her, she insisted, staring in disbelief at Anna as the older woman just laughed. Anna explained that they had had danger come to their building with seven other couples, so what was one more? Anna laughed even harder when Imly stated that she was not part of a couple. Anna had reached to hug her, telling her to just wait, that the men in the building staked their claim on their ladies at their first meeting. Imly finally remembered to snap her mouth closed.

Doc headed for the kitchen, yawning, a hand rubbing at the back of his head. It had been a long day for him, the emergency department where he worked seemingly overrun with patients. He paused at the doorway, his eyes on Brendon, watching as the younger man just sat, his hands folded on the table in front of him, a puzzled look on his face. Brendon had slipped away long enough to his apartment to shower and change, returning as quickly as he could. He was deeply worried about Imly. Doc shook his head. Another one, Lord. Why is it that these young fellows have to meet their ladies when the ladies are in danger? He reached to pour himself a mug of coffee and then filled Brendon's mug again before he started searching through the cupboards.

Anna stood and watched him, a smile on her face, knowing exactly what he has looking for.

"You won't find them, Doc." Her smile widened as he glared at her.

"And why not? You know that I need my sweets."

"I know you do. Sit. I'll get them." Anna reached into the one cupboard that he had not searched and pulled out the container of squares. "Here you go."

"Thanks, love." He looked towards the door. "Imly?"

"I finally convinced her to have a shower. She didn't want to put us to any work, she said. She is adamant that she is leaving tonight. She didn't want to take the clothes that I handed her to wear until I sort of promised that she could pay for them. You know we won't let her do that very thing." Anna poured her own cup of tea and sat beside Doc, her eyes on Brendon, looking around as the door opened and then closed and footsteps headed their way.

Barnabas Carey, chairman of the Barnabas Foundation board, greeted them before his eyes lighted on Brendon.

"Doc?"

"He found a lady in distress, Barnabas, and brought her to us. I don't think he's planning on leaving until he sees her again. Besides, he tells us that his front passenger window needs to be replaced before he goes anywhere."

"And he's to be away on vacation next week." Barnabas moved around the kitchen with the ease of familiarity, finding a mug to fill with coffee, sitting at the table, and reaching into the container of squares that Doc shoved towards him.

Barnabas watched Brendon closely, concerned. He was like that with the other men in the building. What most people didn't know was that the Barnabas Foundation paid the men's wages, freeing up their employers to hire other staff without having to search for funds. It was part of the Foundation mandate, to do this in a way to encourage others. The foundation had been named in part for Barnabas by his father, Bruce, but it was also based on the Barnabas of the Bible, who had been an encourager to Paul.

Brendon finally looked up, surprised to see he was no longer alone. He opened his mouth to speak just as he heard a whisper of sound from the hallway and was then on his feet, moving towards the door. He found Imly standing just outside the kitchen door, her arms wrapped around herself, her hair still wet from her shower. She had a woebegone, lost little kitten look to her that instantly endeared her to Brendon, even more than she already was.

He moved to stand in front of her, waiting for her to look up, his heart breaking for her.

"Imly? Are you okay?" His voice was low, low enough that only she could hear him.

"I don't know, Brendon. I just don't know. I shouldn't be here." She looked up at him, fighting to regain control of her emotions, but losing the battle.

Brendon simply reached to enfold her in his arms, tightening them as she fought at first to free herself before she relaxed against him. He took the blanket that Anna handed him and wrapped Imly in it, surprising her when he simply lifted her into his arms, before he headed back to sit in the kitchen, not letting her go. He cradled her to him, looking up with a word of thanks as Doc set a cup of peppermint tea in front of him.

"Imly tells me that she likes her peppermint tea." Doc grinned at her as she peeked out from under the mess of wet hair. "You'll find that we keep a cupboard with just what our friends like to drink." He seated himself again, pushing over the container of squares. "Here. Help yourself. Anna won't let me eat them all."

She stared at him before turning her head to Brendon, discomfort showing briefly on her face at his close proximity before he nodded.

"Help yourself. They are good. But wait? Have you eaten at all today?"

She dropped her head before she shook it. "Not today. Nor yesterday. I think, I don't know. I think it's been four or five days."

Anna made a sound and was on her feet, heading for her pantry, returning with a container of soup from the freezer.

"Imly, here. I'll heat this. In the meantime, Doc, make the girl a sandwich. She can start with that."

Imly opened her mouth to protest just as Brendon's arms tightened slightly around her, stilling her words.

"It's okay, Imly. Let them. It's part of who they are, caregivers to us." He tilted his head to watch her, seeing the moment she acquiesced.

"Thank you. But it's a lot of work." She glanced around, startled to see Barnabas sitting near her, his eyes on his mug. "I'm sorry."

Barnabas looked up. "What are you sorry for?"

"For all this. I'm sorry. I don't know you." Her voice was soft, a natural softness, that brought a sense of peace to those who heard her.

"I'm Barnabas Carey."

Her eyes grew round. "You're him!"

"I am?" He grinned at her, receiving a wavering smile in return. "But, who is that? I mean. I know that I'm Barnabas, but that doesn't explain what you meant."

"Barnabas, you'll confuse the poor girl." Anna patted him on the top of his head as she moved to set the bowl of soup in front of Imly.

"I did, didn't it?" His grin widened. "I'm the Barnabas, or one of them, of the Foundation. Dad named it after me, in part."

Chapter 3

Feeling uncomfortable at being the only one eating, Imly finally reached for the spoon and dipped it into her bowl of soup, Brendon moving them closer to the table, but definitely not letting go of her. She wondered at that, then shrugged inwardly. He made her feel safe and secure, and she wondered at that, too. No one, not even her father, had that effect on her.

Brendon didn't speak, content that Imly was eating, his heart raised in prayer for this lady. He just knew that he couldn't walk away from her, not yet, perhaps not ever. He sighed to himself. I did it, didn't I, Lord? I found my lady, one in distress, just like the others. I was praying that it wouldn't happen, but I just can't walk away from her. Lead in this, Lord. She's scared, worried, beaten in spirit and body.

Imly finally pushed the bowl and plate away, not able to quite finish either the soup or the sandwich, fatigue weighing down on her. Doc had made her another cup of her peppermint tea, just grinning at her protest that the cold cup would be just fine.

She looked around, finding Anna had moved away, intent on something, just what she wasn't sure. She didn't know that Anna had headed for the spare room, finding brand new sleepwear for her, laying out fresh towels, and then kneeling by the bed, to pray for her new friend. She didn't know the circumstances, but that was okay, she knew. God knew them. All Anna had to do was to pray.

Brendon reached for his mug of coffee, groaning slightly as his phone rang. At some point,

Imly had simply stood up and moved to the chair beside him, keeping as close to him as she could. He scanned his messages, a grin on his face at one of them, Doc watching him keenly.

"Brendon?" When Brendon looked up, Barnabas drew in a breath, seeing the determination in his friend's eyes to keep the lady beside him safe. "Are you still planning on leaving in the morning?"

Brendon shook his head. "No, I don't think so. I had no real plans, after all. I was just going to drive around, find a likely spot to camp, and then move on. I have to have the window replaced and John said he'll have to order one in, that it likely wouldn't be in before Tuesday." He shrugged. "I'm fine with that." He glanced at Imly, finding her watching him.

"You were going to go away?" Imly fought the fear that she felt rising in her.

"I was, but I'm not. You need me here." Brendon raised a finger as she went to protest. "You do. Besides, God hasn't said that I can leave, and unless He does, I stay."

"You believe that?" She knew that was how her father thought and how she had, until the last two weeks. She despaired of ever having that certainty again.

"I do. With every fibre of my being." He shared a glance with Barnabas. "You mentioned your parents. Do they know where you are?"

Imly shook her head. "No, I don't think so. And they will be so worried." She rubbed at her face, and the two men with her could see the worry and stress that Brendon's question had raised. "I need to talk to them, but he took my phone. He smashed it in front of me."

Brendon pulled out his phone again, looking over at her. "What is their number?"

"I'm sorry?" Imly didn't understand exactly what he was asking.

"Your parents' phone number. Do you remember it?" He grinned at her as she stared at him before she remembered to snap her mouth closed, a frown coming on her face.

"I do. But why?"

"Because you are going to call them now, put their minds at rest. Where are you from?"

"From up north, near Sudbury. We live out in the woods, which is how he managed to kidnap me. Do you suppose that they put out a missing person's report on me? Or did he do something to make them think I had gone willingly with him?" She glanced up as Barnabas rose and moved to the hallway.

Barnabas turned slightly so he could watch her, his voice quiet as he spoke with their detective friend, Dallas.

"Dallas? Are you still on duty? Good. Brendon has a situation that we need you to look into. What's that? A lady?" Barnabas began to laugh. "It is. Her name is Imly Dickerson, from Sudbury way. It seems that she was kidnapped and brought her by Lewis Wills. That's right. Kidnapping. Assault. He's beaten her. Doc would be the one to tell you how bad if we can get Imly to agree. That's right. That's how you spell it. Thanks. No, we're at Doc's. Okay. Let me know."

—

21

Barnabas stood for a moment, his eyes thoughtful as they rested on Brendon, before he moved away, sending a group text message to the other twelve men in the building, asking for a meeting in the morning. Brendon needed their help this time. His phone chimed with prompt responses in the affirmative. He knew a couple of the men had planned to leave early in the morning, but this is what their friendship was like. Unless it was life and death that they leave, they simply postponed what they needed to do.

Buckley, the minister in the group, sent a separate message, asking for more information. Barnabas sent a quick reply before he pocketed his phone, walking back towards the kitchen, pausing as he heard Brendon and Imly speaking.

He drew in a deep breath as he realized just how close it had been for the two when Brendon's truck window had been shattered by Wills. Brendon had not mentioned that in front of Doc and Anna, and Barnabas was determined to find out why.

Hearing a tap at the door, he moved towards it, comfortable in letting in whoever it might be. Doc and Anna were around, Doc peeking around the doorframe of his office.

Dallas, the detective that Barnabas had contacted, stepped inside, a question on his face.

"What happened?"

Barnabas shrugged. "I haven't got the whole picture, but Imly has a lot of bruising on her face. She was abducted, brought here, and then somehow escaped, finding her way into the cabinetry shop. Brendon hasn't said much."

Dallas nodded, his eyes finding Doc, who had approached them. "Doc?"

"I need Imly's permission to tell you what all I found, but Barnabas is correct. She has been beaten, not given food, and then running for her life. I have no doubt of that fact."

Dallas nodded, moving slightly so he could watch the couple in the kitchen, seeing Brendon on his phone, his voice quiet, his eyes on Imly as he spoke.

Chapter 4

His eyes on Imly, Brendon hesitated before he glanced at the kitchen clock, noting it was still early evening. He was exhausted, but he knew his emotions were all over the place, given what he had been through and from what Imly had detailed to him. He would need to talk with Barnabas and his friends, surmising that Barnabas had already put out a group text to set up a meeting. That is what he did, take care of them.

Dialling the phone with the number Imly had given him, he listened to it ringing on the other end, ready to leave a voice mail, when a male answered, his greeting abrupt.

"Mr. Dickerson? My name is Brendon Conroy. You don't know me, but I am a new friend of your daughter's, Imly." He stopped speaking as he heard a sound on the other end and then silence. He waited before he spoke again, his eyes on Imly, a hand reaching to cover hers that she was rubbing together. Imly's eyes never left his face.

"Imly? Do you know where Imly is? Do you know where my daughter is?" The voice was broken and full of emotion, her father close to tears.

"I do, Mr. Dickerson. I met her today and she is safe here with friends of mine. I work for the Barnabas Foundation, and she is safe in the building here with a physician and his wife who are some of its residents." Brendon's eyes slid closed as he heard Imly's father trying to control his sobs. He heard a feminine voice in the background. "Mr. Dickerson? I will let Imly have the phone but before I do, I should state that she is in grave danger. My friends and I will do what we can to protect her."

Brendon handed the phone to Imly and started to rise, remaining seated as she shook her head, her own hand reaching for his, her fingers cold as she grasped it as tight as she could. She stared down at the phone before she raised it to speak into it.

"Dad?" Her voice was barely audible and clouded with tears.

"Imly? Oh, thank God. You're safe. We have been so worried. You just disappeared and we didn't know what happened. No note. Nothing. Are you okay, lass?"

Imly could hear her mother as well, and for a moment, could not speak, tears clogging her throat before she could gain control.

"I will be, Dad. Mom. I'm sorry. I'm so sorry. I couldn't stop him. I couldn't get away." She could not continue, the phone falling from her hand as she bent over the table, her head buried in her arms.

Brendon's arm was around her even as he reached for the phone, hearing her father's pleas for her to answer him.

"Mr. Dickerson? We do need to speak about what happened. But first, Imly will need to give a statement to the detective who is waiting." Dallas had moved into the kitchen, quietly fixing himself a mug of much-needed coffee before sitting down across from them. "But what I can tell you is that a man by the name of Lewis Wills kidnapped her, brought her to my town where he is part of an accounting firm, has

—

25

beaten her, threatened her life, tried to marry her, and mistreated her.”

“What? Wills? Of course. The scoundrel. I wondered why he had been hanging around town and then coming out to our place, even with a restraining order against him.” Imly’s father, Ian by name, was growing anger. “We’ll leave in the morning to come but it’s a long drive.”

Brendon spoke quickly. “No, that’s not a good idea. Let me talk to Barnabas here. I’m sure he’ll send his pilot, Andy, and the Foundation plane up there to get you.” He looked up to see Barnabas nodding, his phone already out to call Andy. “In fact, he’s right here and making arrangements. We’ll make sure Andy has your contact information.

“I have to ask. Did you put in a missing person’s report on your daughter?”

“We did, and it was to go province-wide but somehow I don’t think it did. The officer we spoke to seemed to shrug it off, that Imly being an adult meant she had simply walked away without telling us. That is not our daughter.”

“No, sir, I don’t think it is. I’ll have the detective ask around, but he’s sitting here, shaking his head that he never received any word on that report.”

Ian Dickerson sighed. “Somehow, we knew that. The officer is one that has been accused of shoddy work before but always manages to escape without any disciplinary action. This time, that won’t happen.”

Brendon spoke for a few more moments before handing the phone back to Imly, rising and walking away, needing to control the emotions and in particular, the anger, building in himself.

—

Chapter 5

Setting Brendon's phone down finally, Imly swiped at her face, wincing at the pain from the bruising as she hit it. She jumped as a warm wet washcloth appeared in her line of sight before she took it was a murmured word of thanks and sweeping it at her face, relishing the warmth and how it made her face feel better. She looked up, startled to see she was alone with the detective, she thought he was, and looked around, panic beginning to build when she didn't see Brendon.

Dallas spoke. "Brendon is just outside the door. I need to get your statement and then he can come back." He grinned at her. "Now, if we're quick, you won't be long without him near you."

Imly frowned before she nodded, suddenly fatigued. "What do you want to know?"

"Take me back to what happened at your home."

Imly nodded, her eyes raising to catch a glimpse of Brendon, praying for courage to do what she had to, to bring Wills to justice.

"It started about five months or so ago, I think." Her brow wrinkled as her mind returned to the past. "Wills started hanging around town, sitting out in front of the office where I worked, coming in and asking me to go with him for meals, for coffee. It came to the point that my employer didn't let me go anywhere for work on my own. He went with me or he had one of his sons or nephews escort me.

"Dad knew and went and talked to him, with Wills promising to stay away from me, but he never did. We would find cards, flowers, and gifts from him on the front steps or the back porch or on my car. It came to the point that I took a leave of absence from my work, hiding at home. We talked to the police up there and took out a restraining order, but it never worked. He would come and go and not be seen. Even with the security cameras that Dad put it, it wasn't clear if it was him. He disguised himself that much.

"Anyway, about two weeks ago, I think, I had had to go into town for an appointment. When I came out, it was pouring rain and really dark. I hesitated for a moment, and that was all it took. A hand came around my mouth and an arm around me, trapping my own arms to my sides. I fought to get away but couldn't loosen the arm from holding me. I was picked up, carried to a vehicle, dumped inside, my hands bound and a gag over my mouth before I was shoved to the floor of the car and a blanket thrown over me. It wasn't Wills that did this. The man was too strong, too tall, and too young. But I heard his voice from the front seat. I don't know how long I was left like this before the blanket was removed and I was pulled up on the seat.

"Wills wasn't there but there were three other men, one driving, and one on either side of me. We would stop on occasions, I would be let out, but a hand was on my arm at all times. If I had to use the facilities, one of them stood outside the door. I couldn't escape. I tried. I fought them. After a day or so, we arrived here and I was taken to a building outside of town and locked into a room. It was bare, with just a mattress on the floor with some blankets. The attached bathroom only had the bare minimum of supplies. The windows were sealed. I had nothing to break them other than my

---

hands and I tried that. They wouldn't break." She paused at that moment, reaching for the glass of water that Dallas had set in front of her, taking a drink. She tried to compose herself, barely able to.

Imly looked up at Dallas, knowing she needed to finish her statement, but ashamed of what had happened to her.

"Wills appeared the next day, unlocking the door, and standing there, not saying anything. He did this for a few days, many times a day, before he finally spoke, telling me that he wanted the heritage that would be mine. I was shocked, I think, unable to respond at first. When I finally did a few times later of his saying this, I just told him that he couldn't have it. It was a trust that came down to the oldest in the family and could not be passed on. He just laughed, an evil maniacal laugh.

"It was after that he started to hit me." Imly felt her face, feeling once more the blows that she had received. "I tried to avoid them, backing away from him, but he just followed me. Finally, I think it was about four days or so ago, he simply said that we would marry, and when I received my heritage documents, I would sign everything over to him. I knew then I had to escape or I would die. He had no plans to let me live, that much he had made obvious.

"Somehow that night, I shoved at him as he was hitting me, sending him off balance and to the floor. I stood, horrified for a moment, before I turned and fled, finding the stairs, running down them, reaching for the back door, and finding it opening under my hand. I hid for a while, watching as he searched for me before I ran for the road and followed it back the way I had been taken, reaching town the next day.

—

"I hid in the downtown area, seeing his men searching for me. I must have been spotted at one point as I hid near the cabinetry shop. Wills was there. I wanted to go in the front, as I had seen Brendon and thought maybe he would help me. I had heard comments on the street about how the Barnabas Foundation men would help and that Brendon was one of them. I couldn't go in the front door, but the back door opened. I didn't think it should have. I ran in and hid, not knowing if Wills would see me. Brendon found me and was bringing me here. He had stopped for a moment and that's when Wills appeared again. He must have followed us. That's how the window was damaged. He hit it with something. Brendon drove away after that and brought me here."

Imly stopped speaking, her emotions overcoming her for a moment, feeling drained in every way. Her spirit had been beaten down over the past two weeks, and she wondered if she would ever be free of the monster. The memories would linger, driving her awake in the night, to pace, looking over her shoulder for Wills to appear.

Dallas studied her for a moment before his eyes dropped back to his laptop, to scan through her statement, clarifying items as he needed to before he printed it and slid it across the table to her, a pen placed on top of it. He didn't wish to approach her any closer, seeing how close she was to running.

"If you would read through it, note anything we need to adjust, initial each page and then sign the last one and date it, I think that will do it for now." He smiled at her. "It's okay. This is how we'll do it. If I have to have you come into the department, then Brendon will bring you."

Imly stared at him for a long time before she dropped her eyes to the papers, not reaching for them again for long moments, leaving Dallas to wonder if she ever would. She finally began reading, her eyes heavy as fatigue weighed them down. Lord, will this end it? I can't do this anymore. He has taken too much from me, from Mom and Dad. From how many others? She finished signing her name and looked up, finding Dallas reaching for the papers, his eyes on her.

"How many?" Her voice was a bare whisper.

"I'm sorry." Dallas was puzzled.

"How many? How many others? How many others has he done this to?" Imly was on her feet, running from the room, searching for Brendon, finding him standing in the hall, just outside the kitchen door, his arms open to scoop her to him, his head bending over hers as she sobbed heartbrokenly.

Chapter 6

Late that night, Brendon slumped in the corner of the couch in Doc's living room, his mouth against his hand as he braced his elbow on the arm. His thoughts were muddled, some dark, some questioning, some hopeful. He had tried to pray but felt his prayers went nowhere. Doc paused beside him, to set down a fresh mug of coffee, and then tucked a blanket around the younger man, before standing beside him, laying a hand on his head as he prayed for him.

Doc sank gratefully down into his recliner, popping the footrest up, a sigh coming from him. It had been a long day, he decided, and far from over. He was thankful that he did not have to work on the next day. He watched Brendon closely before his eyes moved to where Imly lay on the couch, her head resting on a thin pillow laying on Brendon's lap. Anna had covered her with a soft yellow blanket before she had headed to bed. Doc knew that she was not likely sleeping but instead holding vigil for her young friends. It was what she did. He sighed to himself again. Lord, this is what, the eighth one? Are we going to go through all fourteen of the young men? I mean, I know that You are there, that You have protected them, brought the ladies into their lives that are their soul mates, helpmeets, the ladies that they were looking for and praying for, but to have almost lost some to death? I don't know that we can continue like that. But You are almighty and in control.

Brendon's arm rested around Imly, protecting her from what, he wasn't even sure, but he only knew he had to. That danger was imminent to approach her,

—

but he didn't know if she would let him be her protector. Her actions that night had given him hope. He only knew that she had captured his heart, already. He had laughed when the others had said that was how it was, but he couldn't laugh. Not now. Not when it had happened to him.

Doc finally spoke, breaking into his thoughts.

"Brendon? What are your plans?"

Brendon's eyes turned to him before he shrugged and then gestured with his hand. "To tell you the truth, Doc? I have no idea. All I knew today was that Imly needed someone to protect her, to get her away from Wills. This was the safest place I could think of to bring her."

"She's what, almost 28, she said?"

"She is. Why?" Brendon rubbed at his temple, a headache starting. "Her heritage. That comes to her when she's 28. How do we protect her? She said her birthday is in two weeks. Even with her parents here, that won't protect her from Wills."

"No, it won't." Doc remained quiet for a while, his thoughts muddled, an event totally unlike him. "Listen, Brendon. Don't say anything until I am finished. And when I am, I want you to earnestly pray over what I have to say.

"The only way to protect her is for you to marry her." Doc's hand went up as Brendon opened his mouth. "No, listen, please. As her husband, you would be able to guard her heritage, I suspect. She had indicated by her actions that she needs to be with you, that she thinks you will protect her. She is hesitant with the rest of us, but not with you. You rescued her from danger, and part of her reaction is that she is grateful, but it goes deeper. She sees you as part of her life. I am not saying that you should but it is something to consider."

Brendon's eyes had not moved away from Doc's face as he spoke, the words clarifying his thoughts.

"Doc, those are my thoughts. I have been trying to come up with something, short of that, to protect her, and I just can't. I am not sure if she would ever agree, but we need to do something until we can prove Wills' actions and have him arrested. Dallas is working on that, but he didn't hold out hope that it would be quick. Somehow, I don't think that Wills is working on his own. He didn't strike me as being that smart." He looked down as he felt Imly stirring and then sitting up.

Imly pushed the hair from her face, her eyes on his face, a wonder crossing hers, and then hope.

"You would do that, Brendon?" Her voice was soft, soft enough that he had to lean down to hear her. Doc watched them closely, confirmation in his mind that these two were meant to be together.

"Do what?" He had an idea of what she was asking.

"Marry me? We don't know each other. I didn't think that couples did that." She looked askance at him as both he and Doc laughed.

"It's okay, Imly. A friend of ours, Baird, married like this. His wife, Berneen, married him to save his life. They are very much in love." Brendon just shook his head at the memory.

"She did? Wow!" Imly looked over at Doc to see him nodding.

"That's true, Imly. And our friend, Buckley, who is also our pastor, was taken with them and forced to perform the marriage."

Imly looked back at Brendon, then down at the hand he was holding out. She prayed, desperate to have an answer, before she reached to lay her hand in his, finding his closing over hers.

"I will do my best, Imly, with all my being and with God's help to keep you safe." Brendon made his pledge to her, knowing that his life may well be on the line and that he might not survive, but that was his character and his heritage. His parents had been survivors, living in the Yellowknife Territories, as missionaries there, both meeting their death from illness, leaving him an orphan at age 19. He had been in trade school at that point when Barnabas had approached him about moving to Southern Ontario. He had questioned Barnabas, who merely shrugged, said God told him to find orphans who shared his initials and offer them employment.

Imly finally nodded, surprised when he reached to hug her and drop a kiss on her forehead. She felt safe with him, something that she had not even with her father. Why that was, she wasn't sure.

Brendon stood, a hand reaching for her, pulling her to her feet, before he was still and unmoving, his eyes on the far wall, biting at his lip. He looked down at her, not remembering that Doc was in the room, but that would not have mattered if he had remembered.

"Again, Imly. I will do everything with my being to protect you. Only God knows how difficult that will be." He smiled at her uncertainty. "Now, how be you head off to bed? We'll talk in the morning. Doc or Anna will come to get me if you need me. They have also left a phone beside your bed, unlocked, and it has my name and number programmed into it. Call me, no matter what time, if you need me. Do you understand?"

She gave a hesitant smile. "I do. Thank you." She surprised both of them by reaching to hug him before she reached to fold the blanket, whisper a goodnight to Doc, and head down the hall, Brendon moving so that he could follow her progress.

His head turned as he felt Doc's hand on his shoulder and heard then Doc's prayer for him and him alone. He knew Doc prayed for each of them daily, but this was different. Tonight had changed the course of his life and he would not step back from Imly, not when she needed him.

"God bless you, Brendon. Head off for your own bed. I suspect you'll be here early in the morning." Doc paused, a yawn cutting into his words. "Barnabas said Andy was heading up to Sudbury tonight and would connect with her parents early in the morning. He has taken three security guards from the team with him. Barnabas is taking no chances. Two of them will stay at their place for now, until we can sort out what they want to do. He doesn't think that her parents will be safe nor their property."

"I doubt it will be. Thanks, Doc." Brendon hesitated and then turned and walked away, the door closing quietly behind him, heading for his own apartment and his bed. Only he never made it to his bed. He dropped to his knees instead and spent hours in prayer, before he rose, showered and dressed for the day, and then wandered his apartment, imaging Imly moving around it, assessing what he needed to change. He finally sighed. He would wait until he found out what her likes and dislikes were. He searched for his wallet as the dawn broke, heading for his truck, broken window and all, intent on rousing a friend who had a jewelry store. He had some rings to buy and he wanted to find the right one. His friend was an early riser, Brendon knew, and would not hesitate to open up his store for him.

Chapter 7

Later that morning, Brendon stopped just inside the door of the conference room, his gaze roaming the room, seeing all of the men except for Barnabas, gathered there, quiet conversation, teasing, and laughter filling the air. He smiled. Each one was from a different province or territory, but all had become close friends, dividing without intention into two teams of six, with Breck and Barnabas as their leaders.

He jumped as he felt a hand come down on his shoulder. Buckley stood there, a grin on his face, but concern in his eyes. He had been through similar situations with seven of the men and had prayed that the other seven, including himself, would not face adventures as they termed it.

"Brendon?"

"Buckley?" Brendon mimicked his tone of voice, a grin covering his face.

"Brendon? You too?" Buckley shook his head. "I thought that we told you, seven was enough. The rest of us aren't to undergo adventures."

Brendon began to laugh, bringing the attention of the others to him. "Sorry, Buckley. Somehow, the memo regarding that missed me." He sobered. "I am sure before you ask." He grinned suddenly. "Do you have a date free for us?"

Buckley laughed as well, his own words coming back to haunt him. He had offered dates to two of the couples, only to have his words come back at him from them.

"I do. Today, in fact." He grinned again as he moved away, Breck moving into his space.

"Brendon?" Breck's voice held the concern he felt, his eyes studying his friend closely.

"Breck? She's in trouble, just like the others. I can't walk away from her. She needs me."

"I know you and your heart. You have prayed over this?" Breck watched him carefully. Serving as Barnabas second-in-command, Breck assessed the men on a weekly basis, meeting for prayer with each one.

"I have, most of the night, in fact." Brendon rubbed at his tired eyes. "I have not had God say no. If anything, it's as if He's given His permission and His blessing. Her parents are being flown in today from Sudbury. Andy went to get them."

Breck nodded. "That's what Barnabas said." He looked behind Brendon. "Here's Barnabas now. Let's find our seats, Brendon."

Breck moved away. As Brendon took a step after him, Barnabas' hand rested on his shoulder.

"Brendon? Doc said I should talk to you." Barnabas' voice held concern.

Brendon hesitated and then nodded, a bleak look crossing his face for a moment. "Doc said that, did he? He suggested something last night. Imly had awakened as we were talking. We are going to marry, Barnabas, as soon as we can. I, no, we, need to talk to Buckley about that."

—

"You're sure?" Like Breck, Barnabas had no doubt that Brendon had prayed it through.

"I am. So is Imly. Doc pointed out that I seem to be the only one that makes her feel safe. I know that's no reason to marry, but I can't do anything less."

Barnabas studied him before he nodded. "Another one. Brendon, she has your heart. That I can tell. I watched her last night. It went beyond just feeling safe with you. You make her feel cherished and wanted and loved. She needs that after what she went through. I can't guarantee, none of us can, that it will turn to love, but it's a basis that God can and will work on. We've seen it with Baird and Berneen, for example. Come. Find your seat. We need to spend some time in prayer for all of us but particularly you two. You're setting off on an adventure, and I fear for you both."

The men had broken off into groups of two to pray, a common practice for them. Brendon finally shifted around his chair, his eyes on Barnabas as he sat, his head down, his hands laying on the folder on the table in front of him. No one spoke, knowing that Barnabas would open the discussion when he was ready.

Barnabas finally raised his head, his searching for the seven friends who were married: Baird and Berneen, Benen and Cadee, Blair and Devaney, Bradon and Ennis, Brady and Fynn, Branigan and Guenivere, and Brandon and Hagen. Now, Brendon and Imly. He thought it was heading that way last night, but he didn't expect it to happen so soon.

He had heard from Andy. When they had arrived at her parents' home, the house was empty. The doors were broken in and there were signs that her parents had fled quickly, leaving everything but it seemed their identification behind them. Andy and the security guards were searching, but they needed to speak with Imly to see if she had any idea where her parents would flee to. Andy said there seemed to be a vehicle missing. He had been in touch with Dallas, given that he was involved in the case.

Buckley watched Brendon closely, knowing he would have to have a talk with him. He prayed for him, and was it Imly? He wasn't quite sure on the name, his attention going back to Barnabas as he cleared his throat.

"Fellows, Brendon here has become involved in a situation, similar to what seven of you have gone through. He has rescued a lovely lady by the name of Imly Dickerson, who actually hid in his workroom yesterday to escape the man who had her kidnapped and brought here. There are details that are still being investigated. Dallas is involved and has been in contact with the police in the Sudbury area. Imly was kidnapped by Lewis Wills, who we are all familiar with. I can safely say, I think, that each one of us has had a run-in with him at some point.

"Imly has indicated that Wills is determined to obtain a heritage that she has coming to her when she turns 28, in what I believe is two weeks. He has beaten her and also told her that she would marry him. We have no doubt that she would not survive any length of time.

"Imly has been frank with us, I believe, in stating that the heritage only goes to the oldest in the family. There are other issues that we are investigating that may be related to this." Here, he paused, his eyes on the men, hearing the quiet comments and the subdued anger in the voices.

—

"Andy has flown up to bring her parents back, but they seem to have disappeared. He thinks that they have gone on the run and into hiding, but he's not certain on that. Two of the security guards will stay there and search. One will drive back and search on the way down. Andy is flying back today, but will head back up, if he needs to."

Barnabas waited for questions, but none came. He nodded. He knew the hearts of the men and knew that they would be in prayer for the situation and in particular for Brendon. His attention turned then to Brendon, finding him looking down, his hands rubbing together. He is nervous and uncertain, Lord. Only You can bring him the peace He needs. We need to praise You all the time, but it is so difficult in these situations.

"Fellows, Brendon has shared something with me. I know that he has prayed it through and feels it is the only answer for this situation. He tells me Doc suggested that he and Imly marry. We know Doc. He does not suggest something unless he is positive that God has laid it on his heart to do so. Brendon says that Imly overheard the conversation. Their agreement is that they will marry, and as soon as possible. We need to bathe them in prayer as they undertake what will be a dangerous step, for Imly, but in particular, for Brendon. Wills, from what I know of him, will not take this without a fight. We need to stand together. And, yes, we will be working this, just as we did for each one of you seven. Any questions?" He looked towards the door as a tap came to it, and it cracked open.

Anna appeared, distress on her face, searching for Brendon, who had risen and walked towards her.

"Brendon? Can you come? Imly needs you. She tried to call her parents and can't reach them."

"Certainly." He glanced back at Barnabas, who waved him away, concern on his face.

The men all stood, watching intently as Brendon walked away. They turned in unison to Barnabas, finding him staring at the closing door, a shuttered look on his face, that smoothed away quickly.

Branigan spoke. "Where do we start, Barnabas? We can do some today, but Guenivere and I do need to leave by noon." He paused. "Can the ladies meet with her?"

"I agree. I think they should." Baird spoke up. "Not all of them at once, of course. But who would be best? Berneen, I think, given how we married."

"Berneen, for sure. Cadee? Fynn?" Buckley named two other of the ladies.

"Let Anna decide." Breck spoke up. "I agree with Berneen. But Anna will have a sense of who Imly needs to speak with. And just make sure you spell her name correctly. It's i-m-l-y, Brendon tells me."

Chapter 8

Brendon's footsteps slowed as he approached the lobby of the building, Anna's hand on his arm before she pointed to one side. Both sides of the lobby had a sitting area, with a gas fireplace facing each other. Imly paced near the one area, her arms wrapped around herself, panic in her movements. Brendon's steps picked up speed as he walked towards her.

Imly spun as she heard footsteps, her panic increasing until she recognized Brendon. She flew towards him, her arms around him as his surrounded her, hugging her tight. Anna stood to one side, distress on her face for the younger woman.

"Hey, sweetheart. What happened?" Brendon waited patiently, knowing Imly would speak when she was ready. He was not about to push it.

"I tried to call Dad and Mom. They didn't answer their cell phones. I tried to call the landline. He answered, Brendon. He was in their house and answered their phone. He laughed when he recognized my voice. He told me that he was coming for me, that I would marry him and sign over everything to him."

Brendon felt her tears wetting his flannel shirt as he hugged her tighter before he simply swept her into his arms and headed over to one of the chairs, sitting down, hugging her tight to him again. He looked up at Anna and then at Berneen and Hagen as they appeared, concern on their faces.

—

"It's okay, sweetheart. Andy and the men are searching for your parents. He said that he thinks they're fine. But we need to talk."

Imly leaned back so that she could look up at him, studying his face, seeing the strength in it that she thought she had imagined last night. He had a look in his eyes that said she was important to him, the most important thing besides God, and that he cherished her. She sighed. He fit the picture of the knight that her mother had woven into her bedtime stories. Imly had convinced herself that he didn't exist, but he did and he was holding her.

"We do?" Her voice was soft, with traces of tears lacing it.

"We do. I talked to Buckley just a bit ago. He's our minister. We could be married this afternoon if we had a license. And that we could likely get. I know the clerk at the city hall. He would help us."

"He would?" She just shook her head. "I don't know, Brendon. I just don't know."

"I know, sweetheart. It's a big step." He looked up at Berneen sat down near them. "Here's Berneen. She's the one that we told you about last night, who married Baird to save his life. If you want to talk to her, she's willing to do just that."

"She would? She doesn't know me." Imly jumped as Berneen spoke.

"No, I don't know you, but I want to. Brendon has chosen you to be his family. That makes you part of the Foundation family. We help each other out." Berneen grinned. "I was the first one, so I guess you can blame me for starting it all."

—

45

Imly stared at Berneen, a frown on her face. "I saw you."

"You did? When?"

"Two days ago. You were downtown, helping someone. I almost approached you but I saw Wills looking for me."

"Oh, I wish you had. I would have gladly helped you to hide from him." Berneen grinned at her, seeing Imly beginning to relax. "So, do we talk? If Brendon is planning on marrying you today, we need to do some fast work." Berneen stood, waiting for Imly to stand as well, in no hurry.

Imly stared at her before she turned her attention back to Brendon. "Brendon?"

"It's up to you. It is your decision. If you want to just sit here and let me hold you, I will gladly do that. If you want to go with Berneen, and maybe meet some of the other ladies, then I'm fine with that." He looked up to see Buckley standing beside Anna. "And here is Buckley. He would like to meet you as well." Brendon's tone was gentle, not as one talks to a child, but it held understanding that he knew it was difficult for her. He would let her make her decision and then back her, his voice said.

Imly finally nodded, standing and moving towards Buckley.

"You're the minister?"

"I am. I am pleased to meet you, Imly. We've been waiting for years to do just that." Buckley grinned at her frown. "You see, each of the fellows has not dated or shown interest in anyone until they met their lady. That made each of us anxious to meet the ones who would be chosen. You are a beautiful lady, and

Brendon will take care of you and cherish you." Buckley nodded towards Brendon. "Now, we have to set a date. I understand if you want to wait until your parents can be here, or we can track down our friend, the town clerk, obtain the license, and then you can marry this afternoon. Berneen and Anna will take care of fixing you up, I would suspect."

"That's exactly right, Buckley." Anna's arm came around Imly and Imly leaned against her. "But it is your decision, Imly, just as Brendon has said. Unless you agree, we go no further until you do."

"I think." She turned in a panic, searching for Brendon, finding him right behind her, reaching for her, to gather her close. She finally nodded. "Today, Brendon. I feel doom hanging over us, and I want this over. He will try his best to do something before my birthday, and I can't let that happen. Once I have my heritage, no one can touch it. That much Dad has said. This is the dangerous part."

"Then, sweetheart, go with the ladies. I am sure the other ladies are around and I know Hagen's twin sisters will want to be in on it." He bent, kissed her forehead, and then stepped back, letting Anna and Berneen move in and sweep her away.

"She's anxious, Brendon." Buckley came to stand beside him. "She was in panic mode, Anna said."

"She was. He has her scared. And I can't say that I blame her. We need to pray and pray hard for her and her parents. Wills will try anything, and when he's thwarted, her life will be meaningless to him. I can't let him hurt her."

"No, you can't. Listen, I talked to Eddie. He can access what he needs for us, just needs your identification. Do you have Imly's?"

"I do. She gave it to me last night for some reason." Brendon turned. "I gather you're driving."

"That I am. Let's go get what we need. You need flowers for your sweetheart. Anna called the florist. She's expecting you to stop by. Rings?"

"I have those. Frank opened up for me early this morning."

"Of course, he would." Buckley headed into town, his eyes watching the vehicle behind him. "We have company."

Brendon twisted to look behind him. "And we do. I don't think it's Wills. Imly said he answered the phone at her parents when she called. I need to pass that on to Dallas."

"One of his henchmen then. Now, do you want the ceremony in the church or in the chapel in the building? I would suggest the chapel."

"I agree but I want Imly's opinion on that. I won't make any decisions for her."

Chapter 9

Imly turned to stare at herself in the full-length mirror in Anna's bedroom, not recognizing herself in the long lace-covered white dress, her hair covered by a lacy veil. Sadness wafted through her. Her mother should be here to share this moment. Her father should be the one to walk her down to Brendon. And neither were here. Brendon had sent in her flowers, with a note she had read in private, simply stating that he was glad that she had agreed to be his sweetheart, and signed with all his love. Her fingers had covered her mouth when she read that, not sure if he really meant it. She was scared for him, not wanting him harmed but knowing that it was a real possibility. Wills would not take her escaping from him lightly. She prayed, prayed hard, and then her prayers turned to praise, as she had been taught, praise that God had protected her and provided for her.

Doc watched as she walked towards her, her bouquet in her hands, a sad look flittering across her face. He sighed. He had walked his own daughter down the aisle to her groom, and Imly's father should be the one walking his own daughter to her groom.

Doc smiled as she looked up at him, surprise on her face to find him in a suit and tie, a simple flower on his lapel, confused for a moment.

"Imly. Your father's not here. Will you let me meddle in your special day? May I have the privilege of standing in for him, not taking his place, of course? Will you do me the honour of letting me walk you to Brendon?"

She stared up at him, silent for a moment, tears blinding her before she blinked them away.

"Doc, I don't know how you knew, but yes, I would like that. You have become special to me. Thank you." Imly reached to hug him. "Now, where do we need to be? I'm not familiar with the building."

"Then, my lady, I will show you." Doc crooked his elbow, a grin on his face, as he waited for her to tuck her hand into it and let him lead her away, down to the main floor and then down a corridor to a chapel.

They could hear the sound of music before Doc opened the door, allowing her to glance in before they entered. She was surprised, shocked in fact, at the number who had gathered. She glanced up at Doc.

"They're all friends, Imly. The men from the building. The ladies. Some of our security team. Brendon's employer and his family. You have become part of a large family now. No, we are not a cult but a group of believers who care deeply for one another."

An hour later, Imly stood in the rose garden on the Foundation grounds, the late roses scenting the air heavily as Brendon kept an arm around her, laughing at the comments directed his way, making sure that Imly knew she was part of them now. None of them heard the rustling of approaching bodies. The two men stopped, shock briefly on their face as they saw Imly in her wedding dress, tucked close to Brendon. A few minutes of angry conversation occurred before one raised a weapon, pointing it at Brendon.

Brendon looked around suddenly, feeling someone watching them, but not seeing anyone. A sudden jolt to his body had him flying backward to lie still, Imly falling with him, a scream breaking from her.

The men spun, the husbands shoving their wives to the ground and covering them with their bodies. The security men searched and then headed towards the woods, directly towards the two men who fled.

Brady, a paramedic, crawled rapidly towards Brendon, trusting that he would be kept safe, Doc heading that way as well. They paused, their eyes on Imly, who lay still, shock keeping her that way.

"Imly?" The sharpness of Doc's voice cut through her shock. "Are you hurt?"

"No, I'm not." She twisted in Brendon's limp arm. "Brendon! Oh, dear Lord, please, don't let him die because of me."

"Imly. We're going to take a look at him. Brady here is a paramedic. But we will need you to move." Doc waited patiently as Imly shook her head.

"No, I'm not moving. It's his shoulder, Doc. What happened?"

Brady crawled closer, his hands already assessed the wound. "He was shot, Imly. We don't know by who." He looked up at a sound from her, almost the sound a wounded animal would make. "We'll look after him. He would want you safe. What we need you to do is to crawl towards Breck over there. He's right behind you. He'll look after you. We'll be right behind you, but Brendon would want you to do what we ask you to do."

Imly stared at him before she nodded. "Yes, he would. Please? Don't let him die because of me."

—

She turned, her eyes on Breck as she crawled towards him, fear lending speed to her pace.

Breck wrapped an arm around her and then lifting her to her feet, swept her rapidly towards the building and inside, heading for the infirmary, knowing that was where Doc and Brady would bring Brendon.

Imly paced, fear in her heart that Brendon was indeed dead. She looked up as she heard shuffling in the hallway and then Brendon appeared, a hand clamped to his shoulder, pain on his face, supported by Doc and Brady.

Brendon groaned as he sank down on the bed, his eyes closing from pain before they opened and he squinted, looking for Imly. He beckoned to her, reaching out a hand to her. Imly took it, disregarding the blood that covered it, fear on her face.

"Brendon?"

"I'm okay, sweetheart. Doc and Brady will patch me up. They want to take me into Emergency. Will you go with me? You need to change." His eyes closed against the pain as he bit his lip to keep from groaning.

Imly stood, horrified that he had been shot. She jumped as a hand touched her arm and Anna spoke to her, gently drawing her away and to another room, helping her from her wedding finery and into jeans and a sweater, a wet cloth in her hand to wash the blood from Imly's hand.

Imly stood once more beside Brendon, watching as Doc and Brady worked on Brendon, before he was helped to his feet and walked out to Doc's vehicle, to slide onto the back seat, his head

———

going back on the seat for a moment from the pain,
before he looked for Imly, reaching a hand for her, and
then tucking her close to him.

53

Imly perched on the edge of a seat in the waiting room, her eyes on the door to where she knew Brendon was being assessed. She didn't see the men gathering close around her, to hide her and protect her. Berneen sat beside her, an arm around her, knowing only that Imly needed a friend with her. And Berneen considered Imly a friend, even if she was just a new friend.

Anna sat on her other side, her heart hurting for Imly, her thoughts changing to prayer, watching as Dallas spoke with the men and then the ladies before he approached Imly, pausing to study her before he crouched down in front of her, into her line of sight.

Imly jumped as Dallas suddenly appeared before her, not having seen him approaching her.

"I'm sorry."

"What are you sorry for?" Dallas was puzzled.

"I'm sorry Brendon got hurt. It shouldn't have happened. I brought this to him. It's my fault." Imly refused to look at Dallas, her eyes locked on the door, wishing someone would just come and get her. Doc stood for a moment, watching her, before he walked towards her, standing out of her line of sight.

"It's not your fault, Imly. Brendon knew what he was doing. He would have assessed the risks and made his decision. You were his main concern, not himself. We'll talk more. But right now, Doc is here to take you to Brendon." Dallas rose, letting Doc move towards Imly.

Imly was on her feet, almost running towards the doors, Doc reaching to stop her.

"Just a moment, Imly. I will take you in, but we will be taking Brendon to surgery. The bullet didn't hit anything vital, but it did tear through some muscle. That will heal."

"It will?" Imly shifted impatiently, just wanting to be with Brendon. "But then he can't work."

"That's not important right now. He's worried about you, Imly. He's afraid Wills will have you taken from here. It's a perfect opportunity." Doc paused outside a room, a hand on her arm. "Dallas is taking precautions. Barnabas has brought in some of the off-duty security people to help guard you two, who, by the way, came in willingly. We'll do everything we can to protect you, but you need to stay with one of us or the police, and if we say run, you run."

Imly nodded, her attention not really on Doc and what he was saying. Realizing that, he sighed. *Another lady, Lord, who is so focused on her man that she is putting herself at risk. Protect her Lord. I don't know if we can go through what we did with Bradon and Ennis, almost losing them.*

With Doc's hand on her arm, Imly stood for a moment, her eyes on the nurses as they moved around a stretcher before Doc nudged her forward. She stopped at Brendon's bedside, her eyes only on his face, not lifting to any of the equipment. *He's too white, Lord. What did I do? I brought him to this. I hurt him. I can't do this.* She moved backward, intent on running and hiding, leaving Brendon to his friends. She just knew that she was responsible and hated that.

—

Brendon shifted uncomfortably on the bed, his eyes opening before he groaned, a hand reaching for his shoulder. He searched, looking for Imly, finding her standing near him, but not close enough. He frowned at the fear on her face as well as an emotion showing that he just could not read. His hand out, he beckoned her closer, reaching to grasp hers as she came closer.

"Imly? You're okay? You didn't get hurt?" His eyes narrowed against the pain, but he kept focused on her, ignoring the activity around him.

Imly shook her head. "No, I didn't, but you did. It shouldn't have happened, Brendon. I'm sorry. Maybe we shouldn't have married."

Brendon struggled to sit up, against the protests of the medical staff, his only focus Imly. He wrapped her in his good arm, feeling her struggle when he did so until she relaxed, her arms coming around him.

"It's okay, sweetheart. I knew the risks. God didn't stop us from marrying. He will protect us. We may not like what we have to go through, but He is there. What's the saying? Praise Him in the storms? That's what we will do." His head dropped against the softness of her hair. His voice whispered softly in her ear as he continued. "We met under difficult circumstances, but I would be lost without you." He glanced up and past her as he heard the clatter of wheels and the team from the operating room appeared. "They've come for me, sweetheart. Stick with the men from the building. They'll protect you. They'll also work on solving this. It's what we do."

Imly nodded, unable to trust her voice to speak. Her arms tightened around him, reluctant to let go.

Brendon's voice softened even more as he prayed for his lady, not himself, his prayer turning to praise for God's protection. When he was finished, he paused before he kissed her forehead. His eyes on her face, he nodded. "I love you, Imly. Remember that." With that, his arms loosened and he dropped back on the stretcher, his eyes closing against the pain, giving up the fight to stay alert.

Imly stood, Doc's arm around her, watching as Brendon was transferred to the other stretcher and then wheeled from her sight. She followed as close as she could, Doc walking with her. She didn't see Brady and Barnabas approaching and then walking with her. Doc shook his head at the two men before he directed her steps to an elevator, to walk her into the surgical waiting room and make her sit. Anna was waiting and just swept her into her arms, holding her as she shuddered, unwilling to let any tears fall.

Barnabas watched closely before he turned to Doc, finding Dallas standing nearby.

"Doc?"

"The bullet tore through muscle. They'll repair it. He'll not be working for a few weeks. Once it has healed, we'll get him into physiotherapy. It's Imly I'm worried about. She's about ready to run." Doc tilted his head to watch her. "She blames herself."

"I know she does. They all have." Barnabas spoke quietly. "I heard from Andy. They still have not located her parents, but someone that they talked to mentioned another home halfway between here and their home. Imly didn't mention that."

—

"They have?" Dallas spun. "I'll be back. I still need to talk to Imly." He was away before Barnabas could continue.

Barnabas shook his head even as Brady grinned at him.

"Didn't expect that?" Brady sobered. "Listen. Those of us who had planned to be away aren't leaving. We'll be heading back to the building and the conference room, setting up to research as we have. Does she know Emma, by chance?"

Barnabas gave a bark of laughter. Emma Findlay was well known for tracking down people and addresses and whatnot that no one else could find.

"It would be nice, but I have no idea. See what you can find." Barnabas turned as he heard his name called. Hagen's sisters stood there, Berneen with them. "Girls?"

"Barnabas, does she have any clothes? I mean, of her own?" Hollie was upset, not quite framing her words as she should.

"I don't think so, Hollie. Why? You want to go shopping for her?" Barnabas grinned before he reached to hug each of the twins. "How be you head off then? Berneen, you're with them?"

"I am. I have a good idea of what she wants and likes." Berneen's head turned as her brother, Darbie, spoke from beside her.

"I'm in, too. Breck was looking for you two, Haley. He said something about needing to take you to some stores?"

Haley grinned. "He did? Good." She turned as Breck appeared. "Breck?"

"Here you two are. Come on. I want to go shopping." He winked at them, causing them to grin, before they reached to tuck their hands into his arms that he was holding out for them. Breck was a favourite of theirs and they knew that he was ready to have fun with them shopping.

Berneen shook her head before she grabbed at Darbie's arm.

"Let's go. They'll leave without us."

Doc just shook his head, knowing that Breck would pay for everything for Imly, without saying anything.

"Doc? How is Imly?" Barnabas had turned to watch her.

"That is a good question. The last two weeks have beaten her down, I think. She's subdued, terrified, looking over her shoulder. Now, this with Brendon. He's been the only one to reach through to her and he's not available to her right now. That concerns me. That and the fact that her parents aren't here. What's the story on that? Are they on the up and up or are they involved deeper than we know?" He walked away, leaving Barnabas staring after him.

—

Chapter 11

Late that night, Brendon raised the head of his bed, wincing as a shaft of pain shot through his shoulder. Thanking God that it was not his dominant hand, he searched the room, not finding Imly there. He found the release to the bed rail, lowered it, and then shifted himself to sit on the side of the bed. He glanced around before he stood, waiting until his head cleared before he moved towards the cupboard, finding a pile of clothes that someone had brought in for him. He dressed quickly, leaving the room, searching for Imly, finding her curled up in a chair in the waiting room.

Brendon paused, a smile on his face. She hadn't left him. He had been afraid that she would run, and then he would have just followed her. He looked up to find Benen and Burnie standing nearby.

"You two are here?" Brendon looked around. "Who else is here?"

"Brady. He's getting your discharge paperwork. Doc has taken responsibility for you. Your surgeon said you can leave, unless you would rather stick around here." Burnie grinned before he nodded towards Imly. "Go and find your lady. She refused to leave." He sobered at the thought of the fight that they had had.

"He's right. We tried to get her to come back to the building, promised to bring her back first thing in the morning. She just refused. Branigan was afraid that she would run, hide, and then come back without anyone around here for her. We have word that Wills has men watching here." Benen watched Imly closely before he looked at Brendon.

"So, we sneak out in the middle of the night? Is that the plan? Thinking they won't be watching?" Brendon shook his head before he headed to where Imly was curled up. He sat beside her, his eyes on her before he reached to drop a kiss on her head.

Imly roused, instantly awake, fear running through her before she realized that she was still in the hospital waiting room. She straightened, her eyes finding the two men near the doorway, watching her before they looked away. She sensed someone beside her and jumped, her eyes huge as she stared at Brendon.

"Brendon? You're here? You shouldn't be." Imly tried to stand, to grab for his arm, to try and make him rise and go back to his hospital room. "You're dressed. Brendon!"

"It's okay, Imly." Brendon could not get her to calm down, so he simply swept her into a hug, waiting until she had stilled. "I'm going home. Doc has made arrangements for that. We're making an escape during the night. Wills has men watching us."

"He would." Imly sounded disgruntled. "When will I be free of him?"

"Soon, I pray, sweetheart." He looked up as Burnie approached. "All set?"

"We are and we need to leave now. Brady spotted one of the men heading this way. We're heading for the service elevator."

A while later, Brendon stood in his kitchen, resting his hand on the countertop, hearing soft rustling as Imly wandered through the rooms. Then, he heard silence and turned his head, wondering where she had gotten to. He sighed. He was almost asleep on his feet,

—

the pain medications given him kicking in. He headed for the bedroom, stopping for a moment as he found the bedside light on.

Brendon frowned, stepping back to look into the spare rooms. He didn't see Imly, but he could hear her, muttering softly to herself. He simply shook his head, and instead of heading for bed, he walked to his office, dropping down into his desk chair, reaching to click on the desk lamp, a gift from his own father when he graduated high school.

Dad, you would love my bride, Imly. She's soft spoken, like Mom, but I think I will see a fiery side to her. It has to be, given her deep red hair. Hair like Grandma's. She's the lady that Mom wove into my bedside stories. I love her deeply already, Lord, how I don't know. Help me to protect her, to bring her to safety, to do what I can to reach down and bring her back to who she was. That, dear Lord, has been driven down inside her. Help me to teach her to praise You in all circumstances, no matter what.

Imly stood just outside the doorway, watching him, wanting him to rest but not comfortable enough to approach him. She sighed, sorrow filling her for a moment as she watched him, and she just didn't know why. She turned, heading for one of the spare rooms, to creep into bed, but not to sleep, at least not at first. She listened for Brendon to move around but she dozed off without hearing that.

Hours later, Brendon stood, disoriented for a moment, before he headed for the door, cracking it open to find Breck standing there, Brandon and Bradon with him. He stood back, balancing himself for a moment with a hand against the wall.

"You're here early." He complained as he walked towards the kitchen, squinting at the clock. It couldn't be ten already, could it? "You're supposed to be at church. I'm not going to make it today."

"We know that, Brendon." Bradon simply moved him to one side and reached for the coffee carafe to start a pot of coffee. "We need to talk to you and to Imly as well. Is she up?"

"I have no idea. I just woke when you hammered at the door." Brendon was grumpy, an unusual circumstance for him.

'Sit, Brendon." Breck's voice was stern, not a usual tone for him. "You'll fall over if you don't. And I for one do not want to explain to your bride why that happened." He had noticed Imly hovering in the doorway, not sure if she should come in or not. "Imly? Will you talk sense into Brendon?"

"I'm sorry. I can't do that." Imly turned and walked away, the men hearing a door close softly in the distance.

Brendon stared at the doorway, not sure what had just happened. He was torn, wanting to go to Imly, but also needing to hear what his friends had to say. Brandon finally turned him to the doorway.

"Go, find Imly. She needs you."

Chapter 12

Imly had merely nodded when Brendon had approached her, not turning around, not wanting him to see the tears on her cheeks, the cheeks with the darkening and yellowing bruises. She was ashamed of her looks, ashamed that she had been treated like she had by Wills.

Brendon had given a small sound and then just swept her into his arm, holding her, not finding her struggling to escape. That concerned him. He tilted his head finally to look at her.

"Imly? Please? Don't shut me out." He waited until she nodded. "I will not leave you until I know you are okay. Breck has some information and questions that he needs to talk to us about. Please?"

Imly had had a suspicion that was why the men were there. "But they're supposed to be in church. It's Sunday. It's not right that they are here and not there."

"That doesn't matter. They are where God wants them. Now, let's go see what they are wanting. If I know Bradon, he has probably started his French toast for us."

"He cooks?" Imly was surprised.

"We all do. In fact, we have a potluck supper once a month, just to get together for some fun times, without worrying about anything else."

Breck looked up from the papers that he had spread out in front of him, opened his mouth to speak, and then snapped it closed. His own face grew dark with anger as he studied the bruising on Imly's face before he caught the anger quickly flashing across the faces of the other two.

Imly sat, not speaking, her demeanour withdrawn. Brendon sighed, his hand going to feel his arm. It was beginning to be painful but he refused to take anything. Not yet, at any rate, he thought. Pushing away his plate, not able to finish the meal set before him, he watched Imly closely, before he spoke.

"Breck? I know you. I know Bradon and Brandon. As much as I enjoy your company for breakfast, and it is something new for Imly to discover, that we do like to gather and eat, you are here for more than that."

Breck nodded. "I am. First, Imly. Your parents? Did they have another home or some place that they might have fled to?"

Imly looked up, startled, before she shook her head. "Not that I am aware of. I was raised in that house, Dad saying it was one that had been in the family for a long time. I don't remember his parents or Mom's. They said that they had died before I could remember." She searched Breck's face. "Why? What aren't you saying?"

"That we have not found your parents. Not yet. The men up there have searched. The police have been involved. And no, that officer has not been in the loop at all. We have traced him back to Wills and he is now off duty and will be until he is cleared. He has admitted not passing on your parents' report on you."

"I knew that. What else?" Imly's hand rubbed against the wood of the table until Brendon's hand covered hers, his grasp light but tight enough that she stopped her movements.

"We have evidence that there is another house that they own, between here and Sudbury. There is also a house here in town that is in their name. This is concerning, Imly, that they have these and you don't know about it." Breck's voice, while stern, held compassion for the young woman in front of him.

"I didn't know. I'm sorry. I'm so sorry."

"Don't apologize, Imly." Bradon spoke up. "We have found information on your father. What does he do for a living?"

"Dad? He has a woodworking business. Why?"

"Because the evidence that we have found shows that is not where his income comes from. The heritage you said you had coming? There is nothing like that. There is no clan that they belong to. Not how you would think, that is."

Imly sat back, devastated at the words that she had heard. "If not, then who are they? Who am I? Am I really who I think I am?" She looked up at Brendon. "I'm sorry. I shouldn't have come into that shop. I'm so sorry."

"There is nothing to apologize for. You didn't know. You were raised thinking one thing." His arm went around her in a hug. She didn't see the look of pain that briefly crossed his face. "What else?"

"Jim is heading this way. Dallas is feeding him some addresses. He's searching as he comes." Breck paused, not quite sure how to phrase what he needed to say. "Imly, it is my turn to say I'm sorry. The evidence that Dallas has been able to find is that your

—

father was involved in white-collar crime in Ireland and fled to here. There is a warrant out for his arrest over there."

Imly stared at him. "Then, who is Wills and what does he really want? If there is nothing that comes to me, why do what he did?"

Chapter 13

Barnabas looked around the conference room that afternoon. Sunday afternoon and a long weekend, and the men were here. He could see a few of the ladies as well, Berneen, Cadee, Hagen, and he smiled, Haley and Hollie were there. So were Alice and Farr, Fynn's brother and his wife, Alice being a police officer. He knew that she would have asked for permission to be there from her supervisor.

He turned as he heard footsteps stop beside him. Benen stood there.

"How is she?" He was concerned, knowing that it would have been devastating for her to learn what Breck had told her.

"Breck said that she didn't really react, just asked who Wills was and why he was after her. His gut feeling is what we thought. She had no idea that her father had been involved in crime."

Barnabas nodded. "Listen, how free are you in the next week or so? Can you fly over there? I can give you some names to approach. Something just doesn't ring true with this."

"I can make the time. Cadee will go with me. That would work. Anyone else?"

Barnabas studied the men. "Branigan. Take them with you. Amy will be in tomorrow morning, she tells me. She'll give you what you need. Andy will fly you over and stay there until you're ready to come back. He's fighting mad, he tells me. He saw Imly's face last night."

"Wills was brutal, but so were some of the others." Benen walked away, heading for Cadee, to draw her away from the others, his thoughts dark as he remembered how he had almost lost her to a poisoning.

Breck paused before he entered, his thoughts muddled and troubled. He had spoken with Brendon again, to try and make sense of what was going on. Neither one of them could understand it.

Brendon turned as Imly approached, a woebegone look on her face. He simply enveloped her into a hug, waiting for her to speak, his hand entangling in her hair as it rested on her shoulder.

"Brendon? Why? I'm sorry. That seems to be all that I can ask."

"It's okay, sweetheart. We understand. You don't want to know what the other seven have faced. Bradon was in fact drowned and revived. Ennis was stabbed, and Doc wouldn't remove the knife, which was a good thing. Cadee almost died from a poisoning."

Imly simply nodded. "I see. Wills? He seemed convinced I had something coming to me. How do we find out? Do we need to go back up there?"

"No. Dallas is heading that way, he says. He needs to, as part of his investigation. He stated he would simply pack up everything he thought he would need and bring it back. He has the warrants he needs for that. He's been working with the force up that way. He asked if there was anything you wanted to be brought back."

Imly stared up at him. "He'd do that? Then, my Bible and my laptop. They're on the desk in my bedroom. Tell him if he needs permission, he can bring anything he thinks he needs. Dad has a safe. I'll give him permission to search that. Just let him have the code, that all he needs." Imly thought through what she needed to do. "I guess that I'll need to head that way at some point. Pack my stuff. I won't be going back there, now will I?" She turned to walk away, stopping as Brendon spoke.

"How be we have the men up there pack everything up for you? They can rent a truck and bring it back down with them. Would that work?"

She turned slowly, her eyes on him. "They would do that?"

"They have already offered. In fact, Levi has already begun to gather boxes, just in case. As to cost, the Foundation covers that."

"They can't!" Imly was horrified at the thought. "That's too expensive."

"Imly, I haven't had a chance to speak with you about something. You know of Barnabas?"

She nodded. "I do and I don't know why. I heard Dad talking about him one day, and the name stuck as well as the Foundation name. Why?"

"Because part of what the Foundation does, is just this. They help, without asking. It's part of the mandate to be encouragers. What did you do for work?"

"Me? I was a secretary. Not that I'm going back there."

"No, but Lawrence asked. He's been looking for someone to take over in the office. He's busy doing deliveries, I'm busy in the shop. He's looking at hiring to help with sales and in the workshop. If you want, you can have the work in the office." Brendon paused, biting at his lip. "The thing of it is as well, once we married, you automatically became an employee of the Foundation. It's how they have it set up. The men's wages are paid. When we marry, that extends to the wives. That's part of being encouragers to the couples."

"They do that?" Imly was shocked. "I see. I guess I didn't expect this. Now, what, Brendon? Wills is out there. How do you go back to work, and how do I go about a normal life?"

Chapter 14

Hearing footsteps rapidly approaching from behind him, sounding heavy, Brendon began to turn and step to the side. Before he could, he was slammed into the building wall, deliberately on the side with his wound. His senses swirled as the world around him darkened. He dropped to the ground, his hand on his shoulder, breathing heavily from the pain. The footsteps faded even as other steps were heard running towards him.

Blair and Burnie reached to help Brendon to his feet, letting him lean against the wall behind him. His eyes were closed against the pain. It had been a week since he had been shot, and he had ventured into town, just to see Lawrence and find out where work stood. He had certainly not expected to be ambushed and end up almost flat on his face on the sidewalk.

"Did you get the number of that truck?" Brendon's eyes cracked open slightly.

"No, but we have a description of him." Burnie's hand under his elbow helped Brendon maintain his footing. "Blair headed that way and said he'd make the call. What are you doing here? And is Imly with you?"

"I came in to see Lawrence. I had not planned this, you know. Imly is with some of the ladies, having lunch they said. They are trying to include her, but she's withdrawn, Burnie. I can't even reach through some of the barriers that she has up."

"It will take time. It's been a shock. Being kidnapped, assaulted, escaping, marrying, having her groom shot on their wedding day, having her parents disappear and then finding out she had not been told the truth about them. How does that sound?" Burnie was angry, not at Brendon or Imly, but at whoever it was behind it all. "I don't think that Wills is the brains behind it. He doesn't strike me as having the ability to plan all this."

"Sounds about right." Brendon's hand found his shoulder. "Is it bleeding?"

Burnie shoved aside the collar of Brendon's sweatshirt. "No, and it wasn't for trying. He really hit you hard. On purpose." Burnie's eyes dropped to the ground and he stooped to pick up an envelope. "He dropped this."

Brendon, by this time, had managed to open his eyes all the way. "An envelope?" He reached for it. "And addressed to me." He stiffened his knees. "Can we sit somewhere?"

"Let me have your keys. Blair drove us in. I'm driving you home and this time, you're staying there." Burnie eyed his friend. "That man meant business, Brendon."

Hearing the door close and then silence, Imly carefully peeked out from the kitchen, finding Brendon standing in the hall, a hand braced against the wall. His face was white and pain-filled, and that scared her.

"Brendon?" When he didn't reply, she approached him. "Brendon?"

He looked up, bleary-eyed, before he reached an arm to tuck her against him. "Sweetheart? I didn't expect you to be home yet."

—

"Yeah, well. I am. What happened to you?" She tried to support him as he walked, directing him into the living room. "Here. Sit on the couch." She watched as he dropped heavily down before she was away, fixing his coffee and her tea and then reaching for the pain medication.

Half an hour later, Brendon looked up, feeling slightly better, before he reached for the envelope Burnie had stuffed into his pocket.

"I was knocked down outside of my work, and someone left this for me." He looked over at Imly before he reached to pull her to him. Tucking her close, he fingered the envelope. "He left this for me."

"Wills?"

"That's what we think, but we are not sure. None of us got a good look at him." Brendon sighed. "But, first, how was your lunch?"

"Okay, I guess. I just wasn't in the mood for it. I'm sorry. I still think that I don't belong here."

Brendon sighed. He suspected that was how it had gone. "Sweetheart, you do belong here. All of the ladies have expressed the same sentiment in different ways. I know it's tough." He waited for her to speak. When she didn't, he tilted his head to look at her, seeing once more the woebegone look on her face. "How can I help you? How can I make it better for you? I am praying for you, for your parents. For resolution of this."

Imly shrugged. "I don't know, Brendon." She looked up, her eyes troubled. "I wish I could talk to them, find out what is going on." She poked at the envelope. "You need to open that."

"No, first, my bride needs me to help her. What can I say, sweetheart?" Brendon watched her before he sighed to himself. This is working well, Lord. Now, what? Before he could stop himself, he reached to kiss her, startling both of them. He drew back, mouth open to apologize before he reached to kiss her again.

Imly had been startled with the first kiss, but she welcomed the second one, reading in it Brendon's growing feelings for her, and knowing that she was attracted to him as well. How that was possible in such short a time, she didn't understand.

Brendon finally drew back, leaving Imly with rosy cheeks, and looked down at her.

"I will not apologize, sweetheart."

Imly shook her head. "No, don't." She poked at the envelope again. "Now, will you open that?"

Brendon opened the unsealed flap and pulled out a single sheet, unfolding it. His eyes dropped to the bottom.

"It says your Dad's name."

"That can't be right." Imly leaned over. "That's his name, but not his writing. What is going on? What does it say?"

Brendon began to read. "*If you continue to investigate, you will lead to our deaths and Imly's death. Stop now. Ian Dickerson.*"

"Dad wouldn't word anything like that. Who is this?" Imly stared at the paper before looking up at him. "Brendon, didn't Barnabas say some of the men went to Ireland?"

"He did. They're due back tonight. Barnabas wants a meeting tomorrow." Brendon groaned. "It's Sunday tomorrow. That means on Monday."

"How? They all work."

"We all work, but when we need to, Barnabas pulls us out and in to investigate or travel or whatever it is that he needs us to do. Our employers are all aware this can happen and are in agreement with it."

"That's a strange way to run businesses." Imly sat back once more, surprising herself by feeling content in Brendon's arm.

Chapter 15

Monday morning found all the men gathered in the conference room, wanting to know exactly what Benen and Branigan had discovered. They could read them to a certain extent, and somehow, they didn't think it would be what they had expected.

"Benen?" Barnabas looked over at him. "What do you have to report?"

Benen and Branigan shared a look. "It's not what we were told or what Dallas was told. I don't know who he talked to, but there is no warrant out for Ian Dickerson. In fact, we were able to determine that the Ian Dickerson we were sent to investigate has never stepped foot in Ireland. The description of the man that we were given does not match Imly's father in any way. That man is the one who was involved in white-collar crime. The investigator we spoke to was surprised to see us. However, he was able to shed some light on what she was told.

"In the older days, there was an inheritance that passed to the oldest male in the family. That included lands, jewels, and a certain standing in society. But we were told that is no longer in effect. We were not able to determine, no matter how we tried or asked, when or why, just that it was at least two hundred years since this had been done. Even if it were in effect, it would not go to the eldest daughter. If there were no male heirs, it simply died away. Whatever monies or jewels or land reverted to the town they were resident of at that time."

"So, Wills is after something that he has heard or read about but isn't in effect?" Breck paused, a thought running through his mind. "What if it is a crime family that had set this up? Kept it as a secret society? Kept it running without anyone in authority knowing? Is that possible?"

Branigan nodded. "We asked that. The investigator wouldn't confirm that, but he did say that there were rumours of that happening. We found someone who will look into that for us over there. He was able to give us names here in Ontario to talk to. That would be our next step. He did say that Benen and I should not be the ones to contact them, that we should find someone outside of our group to do that."

"Emma and Abe." Brady grinned. "They would, or one of their men or friends would do that. In fact, I was speaking with Abe the other night, just to get his feelings on this, and I will come to that. He suggested either his Uncle Eddie, a retired officer, or a good friend, another retired officer, Ben, to look into that."

"That would work." Barnabas paused. "Where do we stand right now?"

"Right now?" Brody spoke up. "We have bits and pieces of information. Not enough to even put together a picture of what is going on with Imly. We have heard from the streets that Wills is still looking for her." His attention centred on Brendon. "He knows about you two. I can say that he was not the one who shot you, but someone involved with him did. I spoke with the owner of the accounting firm that he said he worked for. He was never employed there. And would never be, I'm told."

"Strange." Breck looked up from his notes. "Brendon? Has Imly said anything at all?"

Brendon shook his head. "She is at a loss to explain this. She is also at a loss about her parents. That has caused so much anxiety for her. I wish I could find her father and talk to him. The note that we got? It was signed by him, but it wasn't his handwriting. Nor was it her mother's."

"So, they are either being held captive somewhere or have gone into hiding and someone is using that fact to torment your wife." Blair shook his head. "How has Jim made out on his search?"

"He has found out nothing and that surprises him. There have been no sightings at all." Barnabas looked up, studying each of the men. "I would suggest a couple of you head that way, starting from here. He's searching the main roads. Take the back roads and side roads. It's a long shot, but it may pay off."

Bradon shared a look with Burnie. "We'll go, Barnabas. In fact, I can start first thing in the morning."

"Okay. Talk to Amy for what you need." Barnabas paused. "Anything else?"

"Yes. Fynn mentioned that we might want to talk to Emma and see if she can help. She has resources that we don't and she's good at finding the people who want to hide." Brady spoke of a friend's wife.

"Do that, Brady. Now, let's break off and spend some time in prayer." Barnabas closed the folder in front of him, set his pen down, and rose, heading for Brendon, to partner in prayer with him.

Chapter 16

Staring at the late-season, dark yellow roses on the bushes in front of her, Imly stood, deep in thought, not really aware of where she was. She certainly was not thinking of her safety, that was a definite fact. If anyone had asked her what her thoughts were, she could not tell. She started as she heard a sound and spun, a hand to her throat.

Brody simply shook his head. Lord, she's out here on her own, not even watching or aware of what is around her. That's not good.

"Imly?" Brody walked towards her, a hand up to shade his eyes against the late day sun. It was two days since Brendon had been shot and came home.

"Brody? I'm sorry. I didn't hear you." She paused, seeing the look on his face. "What did I do now? I don't understand."

"Just being out here. On your own. Without anyone knowing where you are. Brendon was looking for you, he said." Brody's hand on her arm stopped her forward rush. "He said it's not urgent. I happened to find him in the lobby and said I'd take a look for you." He grinned at her even as his eyes raised to study the area. "This is a nice seating area. The fellows and their ladies use it a lot. We have quite a range of gardens here." He reached for her hand, to tuck it into the crook of his elbow, before he turned them to walk back towards the building.

——

"I know. I shouldn't have come out here." She sighed. "There are just so many rules right now. And I know I will break every one at some point."

Brody laughed. "We all do, but just keep in mind, let someone know where you are, even if it is just the security guard at the desk. He'll come with you. That's not a problem. The fellows that are married? Their ladies have done that. In fact, a couple were taken right out of the building."

Imly looked at him, shocked. "There is no way that would happen. It couldn't." She continued to stare at him, disbelief growing on her face. "It can't, not with the security you have in place."

"It did happen, Imly. That's why the security is stronger. Barnabas and the Foundation Board have insisted on it. Even still, out here?" Brody waved a hand before he reached to open the door for her. "They can come in and get you and then disappear with you without anyone knowing. That has happened as well. We can't fence off the property. It's too big." He suddenly grinned. "When Brendon's better, have him take you for a walk that way." He pointed over his shoulder. "That will take you to Lake Erie. It's quite a view, to look over at the United States, or even when it's stormy, to see the waves breaking against the rocks. And then the sunsets or the sunrises. You Haven't lived until you've seen them."

Imly simply shook her head. "I'm sure that they are spectacular, but right now? I don't think so."

Brendon caught her last sentence and frown. "You don't think what, sweetheart?" He looked over at Brody as he laughed.

"I was telling her about the lake and the views." Brody waved as he walked away.

—

"He was, was he? They are wonderful. We'll pack a supper or lunch one day or even a breakfast and go down there. I've done that many times." Brendon wrapped an arm around her and turned her to one of the seating areas, waiting for her to sit before he dropped down beside her.

"We will, will we? Not yet, that's understood?" She leaned back on him. "Brendon?"

"Hmm?" He shook his head, coming back from his dreams of sitting with Imly on his favourite rock at the lake, watching the sunset, and maybe, if God willed, watching their little ones frolic at their feet.

"Have you heard anything about Mom and Dad?" She sounded desperate, wanting to know where they were.

"No, I haven't. Barnabas or Breck would have made sure that we did if they had any word." His arm tightened on her. "We'll find them, or they'll find us. The fellows are still working their way up north. They've been in contact with Breck."

Imly sighed, her head going down on Brendon's shoulder. "You shouldn't have been hurt, Brendon. That's not right."

"Yes, it is. If I have to give my life to protect you, I will." He paused, biting at his lips. "I love you, Imly. It's that easy. You are my life, right below God. I will do what I need to in order to protect you."

Imly nodded, sadness filling her heart. "I know that, but I don't want you to be hurt again. I don't know that my heart can handle losing you or seeing you hurt once more." She stopped, unsure of how to express her thoughts and her wishes. Her voice was barely audible. "It appears that I love you too, Brendon. But, where do we go from here? We can't live a normal life until this is behind us."

"Not true. We go on with our lives, living them each day to honour God. That's how we do it." Brendon settled back on the couch, his shoulder aching but not like it had been.

Imly had been listening to him, but her attention had been drawn to the outside, a frown coming on her face as she watched a vehicle pull in, before she was on her feet, pulling Brendon up and away from the lobby, stopping in a hallway to watch the front doors, even as they opened and Wills appeared.

"It's Wills! How dare he!" Imly hissed the words, keeping her voice low, the anger and fear evident in it.

Brendon drew her back further, his phone out, a call placed to the security desk and then to the police department. He looked around, desperate to find somewhere to hide with her, to keep her safe. An arm around her, he swept her into the chapel, snapping the deadbolt on the door to lock it.

They stood, leaning against the door, hearing the heavy tread of Wills as he wandered the building. Brendon frowned. That shouldn't be happening. Where were the security guards? Brendon frowned as he heard the heavy steps hastening away, towards the back of the building.

Imly leaned against him, her eyes on the door, a frown on her own face, before she looked up at him, the frown changing to a question. Brendon shrugged. She reached up to whisper in his ear.

—

"Did he leave?"

"I think so." Brendon listened to the noise outside. "We'll wait here until they come and get us." He turned, the fading adrenaline causing him to stagger, Imly's arms out to catch him and help him to a pew. He sank down gratefully, pulling her down with him, to tuck her against him.

"Brendon?"

"Imly?" He gave a quick grin, causing her to frown at him again. He sobered. "I know. He came right into our home building. He shouldn't have made it down these hallways. Security should have stopped him."

Chapter 17

Brennen and Breck stopped at the chapel door, frowning that it was closed. They knew Dallas was around, coming out when the call about Wills being on the premises went in. Will Peters, the police chief of the town, and also a good friend, had appeared along with him, walking through the building. They had not found any sign of Wills, but they had found his vehicle in the parking lot.

Breck turned the knob on the door, surprised to find it locked, an unusual circumstance during the day. He dug out his keys, the frown deepening on his face. They had searched the building for Brendon and Imly, even as far as Breck entering their apartment, but not finding them. This was the last room in the building that they could search. He shoved the door open and stepped in, surprised to find no one in there.

Brennen stepped in as well, searching, before he stooped, to pick up a phone.

"This is Brendon. He wouldn't have gone anywhere without it."

"Not on his own, that's for sure." Breck walked through the chapel, opening the doors to the cupboards before he paused at the outside door. "They must have gone out this way. And it's hidden to the security cameras." He shoved open the door, stepping outside, then stopping and turning back to the door. "It was not locked, and it always is."

"I don't like it that we found Peter unconscious behind the security desk. He took quite a heavy blow." Brennen stepped out after Breck. "Someone took him down from behind, while he was on the phone. I don't know that he was able to put through a call to the head office."

"No, he wasn't. He hadn't had a chance to even call." Breck walked around the building, searching for just what, he wasn't sure.

Brennen kept pace with him. "I don't understand it. They should have been in the chapel. Unless someone took them from there."

"And that is exactly what I think happened. But who?" Breck stopped in from of the chapel door, his finger touching the lock. "This isn't marked. They had to open it for whoever it was."

"Brendon wouldn't do that for just everyone. He would have had to be certain of whoever it was." Brennen was frustrated and suddenly afraid for the couple.

"I know. Unless it was Imly's parents, and she let them in."

"But that doesn't explain why Brendon's phone was there. Did you see Imly's?" Brennen used his shirttail to pull open the door. "I didn't see another phone."

"I think that it was likely hers on their kitchen table. Brendon had commented that she was refusing to carry one, afraid that Wills would find out the number and keep calling her."

"That's not helpful." Brennen bent to look under the pews on both sides of the aisle, before he stood, a hand rubbing at his cheek. "I don't see anything. Can you access Brendon's phone?"

—

86

Breck shook his head. "Not likely. He told me that he had it secured so that no one could access it."

"That's no help." Brennen turned as the door to the hallway opened and Will, Dallas, and Barnabas appeared.

"No sign of them?" Will's keen eyes scanned the room.

"No, but we found Brendon's phone. And the outside door was unlocked." Breck held up the phone. "I can't access it."

Will and Dallas shared a look before they headed for the door and then disappeared through it. Barnabas watched them before turning to the other two, hearing the door click shut.

"We need to meet. The others are gathering in the conference room. The ladies are arranging to bring in food for us all. It will be a long night." Barnabas ran his hand through his hair. "I don't like this. I heard from Brody. They talked to a police detachment halfway there. Imly's parents' car was found in the ditch near that town. No sign of them. The officer couldn't tell if there were any signs of violence. There wasn't anything in the car, but that was the feeling the guys had when they searched Imly's home. There didn't seem to be anything missing."

Breck shook his head. "First, her. Then, her parents. Now, Brendon and Imly. How do we even know that the incidents are related."

"We're assuming that they are but you are correct, Breck." Will spoke from behind him, causing him to jump. "Sorry. I didn't mean to startle you. Dallas is heading up that way now. He's gotten the statements that he needs." Will looked around, puzzled. "I don't see Brendon just leaving with whoever it was."

"No, he wouldn't. Not unless Imly was threatened. And that is likely what happened." Brennen's words had a bite of anger to them, unusual for him. "And just how do we find them?"

"That I can't answer, fellows, but we need to clear this room. The crime scene techs are heading this way."

Barnabas nodded. "Let's meet in fifteen in the conference room. We need to start making some plans. Those of us who are here."

"The fellows are already there. Brady was reaching out to Abe and Emma, but he said he was having trouble reaching them. He wasn't sure, but he thought this was the week that they usually took off and found Emma's mountaintop and her eagles."

"Is that right?" Barnabas shook his head. "Well, I guess that's that."

"Not quite. Brady did speak with Jace at her business. He's starting a search, but he said Emma was much better at it than him."

"We'll take what we can get." Barnabas held the door to the conference room open before he stopped. "I just had a thought. Would her parents have landed here already?"

Breck and Brennen shared a look before Breck spoke.

"That's a possibility. How be Brennen and I head into town, see what we can find out?" Breck was already moving away from the door, Brennen keeping pace with him.

—

Chapter 18

Two days later, Buckley raised his head from his sermon notes, listened, and then shook his head. He was alone in the church, or so he thought he was. Hearing a sound again, he once more raised his head. Staring down at his notes, he sighed. He was struggling with this sermon, trying to write the words God was giving him on how to praise in the storms, but it just wasn't happening. He sighed once more, threw down his pen, and rose, a prayer on his lips that he really was alone and he could return to his study of the passages that he felt he was to use.

Buckley stood for a moment outside his door, looking down the sanctuary towards the main entrance but not seeing anyone. He frowned. He knew the sound of the front door as it had a very distinct noise when it opened. It hadn't been fixed, at his request, as it alerted him to an intruder if someone did enter the building.

He walked towards the front of the building, searching each row of pews before he stopped, shock on his face, a shout dying on his lips. He sprang forward, dropping to his knees beside the huddled form, reaching to turn the face up.

"Imly? Dear Lord, thank You for bringing her home. Imly? Can you hear me?" Buckley tried to elicit a response from her but to no avail. He reached for his phone and then muttered to himself. He had forgotten it at home that morning, shrugging it off at the time, knowing that he had the church phone he could use.

Buckley rose to his full height, staring down at Imly, torn between running to call for help and not leaving her. Not leaving her won. He reached to gather her into his arms, finding no resistance from her, and elbowed his way through the door, shoving it closed. He shifted Imly around enough in his arms that he could reach into a pocket for his keys and lock the door before he was almost running down the few steps to his car. Wrenching open the door, he carefully set her down, fastened her in, and then slamming the door, he ran for the driver's side. His own door slammed behind him as he headed away rapidly towards town, his glance shifting between the road and Imly.

Parking in the designated clergy spot at the hospital, Buckley twisted in his seat, praying that Imly had responded. She had not, he sighed, and that concerned him. He was out of his seat, around to wrench open the door once more, and gather her close, almost running for the entrance. Surprised looks shot his way before the charge nurse was on her feet, heading for an empty room, Buckley following close behind her.

Doc watched from where he was reading a chart, a frown appearing on his face, before he turned his attention back to his patient. Whoever it was that Buckley had brought in would have to wait. There was nothing he could do about that.

Doc finally moved to that room, his hand reaching for the chart, his eyes on Buckley. Buckley had refused to leave, and the nurse had simply nodded at his explanation. It was not the first time that Buckley had stayed with a patient.

Frowning, Doc looked down at the chart, his steps halting as he read the name before his eyes shot to the bed, and then he was moving rapidly towards it.

—

"Buckley? What on earth?" Doc was already reaching for his stethoscope from around his neck.

"She just appeared in the church, Doc. I couldn't get her to respond. So I have no idea what is going on."

"I see." Doc looked towards the door. "Brendon?"

"She was by herself." Buckley was torn. He felt that he needed to stay with Imly, but he also knew that he had to report it.

"Go, make your calls."

"Yeah, that. I'll have to see if I have change. I forgot my phone this morning." Buckley was frustrated as he dug into his pocket, finding no change.

"Here. Use mine. I'll come and find you when I'm done here." Doc handed over his phone and then motioned him away.

Buckley hesitated, one last glance at Imly, before he turned and walked away, already dialing Barnabas' number.

"Doc?" Barnabas answered in a distracted manner.

"It's Buckley. I had to borrow Doc's phone. Imly showed up at the church just a few moments ago. She's here in Emergency." Buckley held the phone away from his ear at the exclamation from Barnabas.

"Imly? She's there? Brendon?" Barnabas was on his feet, waving at Amy as he passed her desk, heading for the conference room. Bradon and Burnie whom he had sent north were on their way back, just hadn't reached home yet. He shoved the door open hard enough that it startled the men gathered inside, causing them to rise to their feet.

"No, no Brendon. And she's not responding. Doc's with her. I am thanking God that he was here today." Buckley paced, unable to sit.

"Okay. We'll head in. Brady said Abe or Emma were heading this way, or else he was sending someone with material for both us and Dallas." Barnabas stopped his words. "Dallas! Have you called him?"

"Not yet. You were the first. She'll need some of the ladies. Anna for sure."

"They will all want to come, they have been that worried. Call Dallas and then call me back if there is word before we arrive."

Buckley finally ended his call with Dallas, unable to supply much more information than what he had given to Barnabas. Dallas promised to head over as soon as he could, but at the moment, he was on the scene of another crime and he couldn't promise when he would be free. Buckley had simply told him to come when he could, that he doubted Imly would be leaving any time soon.

He looked up as he heard Doc's voice, rising from where he had been sitting, before Doc approached him, pointing to the chairs.

"Sit back down, Buckley. I need to. At least for a few moments." Doc sank down with a sigh of relief, his eyes closing for a moment, before he spoke. "Any word on Brendon?"

"Not a one. He wasn't with her. Dallas was having officers head over to the church." Buckley groaned. "And I locked the door. They'll need to get inside."

"Not right away. One of them can come to get you when they need to." Doc's eyes slowly opened and he rubbed at them. It had been a long day, he thought, busier than normal. He would not leave the hospital until he knew what was going on with Imly.

—

Chapter 19

Doc paused in the doorway to Imly's room, his thoughts on Brendon, before he began to pray. Imly was in critical condition, that much he knew, and he just didn't know who to turn to if she needed more treatment than what they had planned. He turned as he felt a hand on his shoulder.

Barnabas and Breck stood on either side of him, sober looks on their faces.

"Doc? What can you tell us?" Breck knew how careful Doc was about saying much about patients.

"It's difficult, Breck. Her parents aren't here, nor is Brendon. They would be her next of kin, I suspect. If she needs further treatment, who authorizes it?" Doc walked forward, to stop by the bedside, his hand automatically reaching for his stethoscope. He finally wrapped in around his neck again, his hands reaching to feel at the side of her head, a frown on his face.

"She's had X-rays, fellows. There is a hairline fracture on this side of her head. How serious? That we can't tell until she awakens."

"And we don't know when, is what you're saying." Barnabas blew out a breath. "So, where does that leave us?"

"Nowhere." Doc's words were abrupt, from his frustration and fear. "All we can do right now is pray for her. And even at that, I can't guarantee what the outcome will be. God alone knows."

Breck had turned slightly as he heard a sound at the door and then beckoned Berneen in.

"Doc. Berneen's here."

Doc shot her a glance. "Berneen. Has she said who her power of attorneys is?"

"No. We never talked about that." Berneen stood at the foot of the bed, her eyes on her friend. "Doc? How bad? Or can't you say?"

"She's critical, Berneen. I can't go into the details. I have to talk to Barnabas and Breck, but she is under the Foundation care, so that is necessary." Doc watched Berneen closely. "Berneen, will you stay for a while?"

"I can, Doc. That's what I'm here. Baird is waiting outside. I think that he wanted to talk to either Barnabas or Breck."

Breck nodded and walked away, searching for Baird, finding him standing in the waiting room, staring out the window into the darkening sky.

"Baird? You were looking for us?"

Baird nodded. "I was." He drew a deep breath. "I heard from Dallas. It's not good news. He was trying to reach one of you two." He turned, a devastated look on his face, before he swallowed hard.

"Brendon?" Breck's voice was barely audible."

Baird shook his head. "No. Her parents. The authorities up north found them." Baird's words cut off, his emotions getting the better of him. "I should say, they found their bodies. They had never left their property. They were hidden in a shed, and the authorities just found them, doing a more thorough search."

"What!" Breck was shocked, to say the least. "Dear Lord, You will need to comfort Imly. This is not what we had expected."

"No, it isn't. They are looking for Wills now. Dallas said that there was evidence he was involved in it. That day that he answered her call? He was there, but they were already dead. They think that their car was driven this way and then dumped to make us think they were heading this way. It just gets more strange." Baird turned, looking towards the hallway. "How is Imly?"

"Doc's not saying much, but he did say that she is critical. We need to pray, Baird. We also need to find Brendon. I fear for his life."

"You and me both." Baird sighed. "I prayed none of the rest would go through what some of us did. I'm not the same person that I was. It's not possible to go back to that." He nodded towards Imly's room. "She not likely is. And I know Brendon won't be." Baird was frustrated. "How did she end up at the church, anyway?"

"That we don't know." Breck looked around as he heard footsteps. "The rest of the fellows are here. All of us." He frowned as he studied Bradon and Burnie. "How do we tell them that they were on a wild goose chase?"

Bradon stopped near Breck. "Breck? You've heard?" Sorrow flickered across his face. "Dallas called when we were halfway home."

—

"We have. I'm sorry, fellows."

"Not your fault. You didn't know. None of us did." Burnie looked around. "Brendon?"

"No sign of him. And it's not looking good for Imly." Breck opened his mouth to speak, snapped it closed, and walked away, leaving the men staring after him before they exchanged glances.

Hearing new footsteps, Baird looked once more towards the doorway, a frown on his face before he moved through the men, bypassing the ladies who had gathered, and stopped in front of the couple who stood there. He has to be an officer, Baird thought.

"Can I help you?"

The man nodded. "I am looking for either Barnabas or Baird."

"I'm Baird."

"I'm Lieutenant Doug Foster. And this is my wife, Darcie. Emma sent me this way." He reached to shake his hand.

Baird's eyes narrowed. "Emma sent you? Is that correct?"

Doug grinned. "She did. She said you would question whether I was legit or not." He continued to grin even as Darcie shook her head.

"Don't pay him any mind, Baird? May I call you that?" At his nod, she looked around him at the waiting room. "This is all of you? We were told at your building that you were here but now why."

Baird's face grew grave. "We are. Imly, Brendon's wife, is here. She showed up today, critically injured. There is no sign of Brendon."

Doug frowned. "I'm sorry. I'm not following what you mean."

Baird sighed. "Let's have a seat. Barnabas will be around shortly, I suspect." He waited until they were seated before he continued. "Brendon and Imly disappeared two days ago from the chapel in our building. Imly showed up today in our church. Buckley found her when he heard a noise in the building. There was no sign of Brendon." He paused, sorrow crossing his face.

"Baird?" Darcie reached to lay her hand on his wrist, her eyes raising to Berneen as she sat down beside her husband, an arm around him.

"We received confirmation today that her parents are dead." Berneen leaned her head against Baird's shoulder. "They were missing."

"Oh, no!" Darcie stared at Berneen before she looked down at the notepad and pen that Doug was waving at her. "Thank you, my love. Okay. Talk to me. Tell me everything that you can. Each one of you. And I want to talk to Doc, is it?"

"That is correct." Baird was puzzled, before he looked up at Doug, finding a smile on his face.

"It's okay, Baird. Darcie owns an arts and craft store and has one online, but she was trained as a forensics psychologist. She can do a profile for your detective, without having much information. And I can guarantee you that it will be spot on. She did it for us."

"She did?" Barnabas had slipped into a seat beside Berneen. "Darcie? I've heard of you. Your material is still used for teaching."

"It is? I didn't expect that." Darcie was lost to them after that comment.

Doug simply shook his head and then nodded at Barnabas.

"Where can we talk?"

Barnabas looked around. "Follow me. There's a conference room just down the hall. Baird, make sure Breck knows where we are. I assume the ladies are waiting here."

"We are. We'll keep Darcie company." Berneen smirked at him. "Go. Figure this out. We need to find Brendon for Imly, and it's not happening with us just standing around here in this waiting room."

Chapter 20

Her head moving restlessly, Imly grimaced with pain, but also with the memories that were flooding her mind, destroying the peace that she needed to have in order to heal. She licked at her lips before she turned abruptly to the side of her head that was injured. Pain flashed through her, drawing a moan from her, and then her movements stopped.

Cadee was watching her closely, reaching to press the call button for the nurse, her hand then resting on Imly's. Distress coloured her face. Lord, we need her awake, but it doesn't look as if it's going to happen. How do we praise in times like this? How do we? We can't on our own. That's not how we are. But You can do that in us. You can bring us to praise you in whatever situation we find ourselves.

The nurse entered on almost silent shoes, pausing for a moment to study the monitors, before she reached to take Imly's vitals.

"She was moving. I thought that she was waking up. Then, she turned wrong and stopped moving." Cadee's voice was barely above a whisper.

"She hit the wrong spot, is that what you're saying?" At Cadee's nod, the nurse reached for Imly's chart, to make her notes. "She will be restless. Doc expected that. Doctor Watts is on duty today. I'll let him know. Doc said Dr. Watts would be taking over her care, now that she's on a floor."

Cadee nodded, not taking her eyes from her friend. "Who is in the waiting room?"

The nurse laughed softly. "A better question would be who isn't. All of you ladies, the twins, Darbie, and some of the men from there. There is also a police lieutenant and his wife from outside the area. They were around yesterday but Haven't left yet."

"Doug and Darcie. Good. They can help." Cadee's heart was sore for her friend. "Is Benen out there?"

"He is. I'll send him in, if you like."

"Please." Cadee just needed her husband, to have his arms around her, and to hear his prayers. She knew that others were praying for their friends, but sometimes, she thought, it didn't seem that their prayers went very far.

Benen hesitated for a moment, his eyes on his wife, before he was beside her, his arms around her. His eyes then sought out Imly, a frown coming across his face as he studied the fading bruises on her face but the new enlarging purple colouring on the side of her head.

"What happened to her, Benen?"

"That we don't know, Cadee. We Haven't been able to even figure out how she made her way to the church or from where."

Imly stirred once more, hearing voices near her. She squinted as her eyes opened before she sighed and drifted off again, the pain in her head driving her down into darkness. Her lips murmured Brendon's name even as a tear crept down her cheek.

Cadee leaned closer, horror crossing her face as she heard Imly's whispered words. She spun, her arms around Benen as she clung to him.

———

Benen's arms tightened around her. "Cadee? What did she say?"

"Oh, Benen." Cadee's voice was thick with tears. "She thinks Brendon is dead. That he was killed because of her."

"Oh, no!" Benen looked around as the physician entered. "We'll need to leave, Cadee." He turned her towards the door before he stopped to speak with the physician. "Cadee heard something Imly said. She was alert for a moment and muttered that she thinks her husband is dead, killed because of her."

The physician nodded, a sober look on his face. "That's what we've wondered. Until it's confirmed, we must keep up our hope and hers."

His arm around Cadee, Benen walked back towards the waiting room, knowing their friends would ask how Imly was. And that he couldn't say. Not yet. Cadee stopped, bringing him to a stop as well.

"What do we tell them, Benen?"

"The truth, I guess. We can do no less." Benen hugged her tighter, his eyes on Barnabas as he walked towards him, Doug beside him.

"Benen?" Barnabas' voice held the question that he would not ask.

Benen shook his head, sorrow wafting across his face. "Imly had roused but not enough to know that we were there." He paused, his eyes on Cadee, who still hid her face against him. "Cadee heard her say something that is upsetting."

"And that would be?" Barnabas waited for Benen to speak, finally opening his mouth to question him further when Benen spoke.

"Cadee heard Imly muttering that Brendon was dead, killed because of her." Benen paused, a bleak look around his eyes. "How do we prove that he isn't? It's going to be hard enough for her to find out her parents are dead, let alone having to deal with this."

Doug had been listening closely. "How sure is she?"

Benen shrugged, his eyes on the others who had gathered close. "I don't know for sure. We won't know until she wakes up completely and the Lord alone knows when that will be."

Benen looked past Doug as Darcie as she paced. "What's with your wife?"

Doug shrugged. "She's thinking. She does it best lately by pacing. Just so you know, she was treated very badly years ago and that affected her wish to continue in her chosen line of work. She rarely goes back to it, only two or three times. Once was when we reconnected and went through a horrible situation that almost took out our town." Doug looked past Benen. "Is that the detective that's investigating this?"

Barnabas nodded. "Dallas. He refuses to let us use his last name. Doesn't explain that."

Darcie spoke from beside Doug. "No, he doesn't have to. Is there somewhere we can meet? I think we need to get out of the way here and do some brainstorming."

Doug sighed, even as he reached to shake Dallas' hand, realizing they had met a number of years ago. "Dallas. Good to see you again."

"Doug? I didn't realize you knew these fellows."

“I didn’t, not until yesterday. Abe and Emma
sent Darcie and me over. You’re the one I have a stack
of material for.”

Chapter 21

A week later, Imly lay back on her hospital bed, her arms crossed across her chest, not willing to look at anyone. She had done this, she thought. She had brought devastation to this group of friends. The ladies of the building had been in and out for the last few days, each one taking the time to spend with her, praying with her as she would let them.

Her eyes closed as her head dropped to the pillow, the nagging headache not letting go of its grip on her. She was frustrated, to say the least, unable to state where she had been, who had taken her, or even how she had managed to escape. Or even, she thought, that she had been released for some reason. Her heart hurt as she thought about Brendon, convinced that she was a widow. She could hear the words drilled into her brain that last night, that he was dead and it was all her fault. Flashes of a picture showing him on the ground, his eyes closed, a large red stain on his chest, haunted her. Imly frowned as she pondered it. There was something off about the picture, but she just could not think of what it was.

Barnabas turned from the window that he had been standing in front of, watching Imly's reflection in the glass, not seeing the coloured leaves on the trees outside or the clouds scudding across the blue of the sky. He was concerned, to put it mildly. Doc had not been able to tell him much, but he had indicated that Imly would need at least six weeks to recover. And that was being generous. They needed to do something to find Brendon and bring him home, Doc declared, not convinced that he was dead.

"Imly? What can we do for you?" Barnabas leaned back against the window, his hands resting against the window sill.

"I don't know, Barnabas. Everyone asks me that, and I don't know." Her head raised as she squinted towards him, the light hurting her eyes. "What can I say? If I had not hidden in the workshop, Brendon would not have found me and he would still be alive."

"Not necessarily, Imly." Barnabas shoved away from where he had been standing, to pace over to take a seat in the chair beside her bed. Buckley, you need to the one giving this talk, not me. "God has control of this, Imly. Not us. Not whoever it is."

"I know that in my head, but it's my heart that's having the trouble." She sighed. "I just wish it was different." Imly looked down at her fingers plucking at the blanket. "Is it really true about Mom and Dad?" Her voice was barely audible.

"It is. I'm sorry, Imly. We couldn't have prevented that." Barnabas leaned forward, his elbows resting on his thighs. "The coroner says that they were likely killed not long after you spoke with them. There is not a lot of evidence that the police are releasing out to anyone, other than Dallas and the team here."

"I know." She bit at her lip even as she blinked rapidly, the headache intensifying. "I just wish it was different. Have we learned anything else that you can share?"

Barnabas shrugged. "Not a whole lot. We know it wasn't your parents that were involved in the insurance fraud and black market sale of those items. Dallas says that he is investigating someone but won't say who. Our fellows are working round the clock right now. And Fynn's friend, Emma, is throwing information at us almost too fast for us to read. Doug's Darcie left a profile for us and passed that on to Dallas."

Imly's eyes narrowed, not altogether from the headache. "Can I see it?"

"You can, once you're released. The physicians won't let you leave right now." He grinned. "Feeling caged?"

Imly stared at him, her face whitening to the point that it startled Barnabas and had him on his feet, reaching for the call button. Imly's hand stopped him.

"No, don't call. It's what you said."

"What did I say?" Barnabas thought back over his words and really wasn't sure which one she meant.

"Cage. I was in a cage of some kind. Not in a house. An outbuilding. A shed. A barn. A cabin. I couldn't quite see what it was, it was dark. And they didn't let us have any lights. Brendon was taken away before I was locked up. I don't know where they put him, but I know that he was fighting them, to try and get back to me." Imly blinked rapidly. "It was early the next morning, I think, that they told me that he was dead and that it was all my fault. They left the cage door unlocked. I think that was done on purpose. I tried to get away, but someone shoved me and I fell, hitting my head, I think, against a rock." She looked up. "Is that when I did that?" Her voice, naturally soft, was barely audible.

"More than likely. It is a miracle that you were able to make your way to the church. We still Haven't figured out which way you came from."

Barnabas studied her, hoping that she would or could remember.

"Barnabas, when can I leave?" Imly eyed the door, ready to jump from the bed and run from the room. "I need out of here. How many?"

Barnabas frowned as he rose to stand beside her, his hand resting lightly on her wrist. "How many? How many what, Imly? I don't understand."

"How many days? How long have I been here?" She was getting more and more agitated.

"Seven days. Why? Is that important?"

"It is." She shifted away from him, off the bed and heading for the door, a hand held to her head in an attempt to control the pain. "I need to leave. Something is to happen today. And I just can't remember what."

Barnabas stood, dumbfounded that she was walking away, no almost running, he thought, before he was after her, a hand out to her arm to stop her.

"Imly, you just can't leave. Not with the head injury that you suffered."

"I have to, Barnabas. I have to go home. Something is going to happen and I don't know what or how to prevent." Imly was almost in tears, not seeing the physician and Doc heading her way.

"Imly?" Doc's voice barely broke through her agitation, and he turned to Barnabas for an explanation.

Barnabas shrugged. "She's convinced that she has to leave, that something is to happen today. Only she can't remember what."

Chapter 22

Pacing the apartment, unable to settle down into a chair or even to lay on her bed, Imly searched for any sense or hint of Brendon. She swiped at the tears trickling down her cheeks. She did not cry. Ever. Never ever. She seemed to be doing that lately, she thought. Imly was grieving, for her parents, for Brendon, for his friends.

Pausing at the French door to the balcony, Imly rested her hand against a windowpane, feeling the coolness of the glass. My life is like that, was her thought. My life and my heart. Lord, how do I go on? How do I live, knowing that I brought this to Brendon, to his friends, to my parents? I just can't go on, not with that burden. Brendon would tell me I need to praise You, but I can't. Not yet, anyway. Lord, is he really dead? Something isn't right about that picture.

Hearing a tap at the door, Imly sighed. It had to be one of the guys, she thought, or one of the ladies, or Doc, or Anna. She didn't feel hospitable right now, not wanting to be around anyone. The tap sounded again, and she finally moved to walk through the living room, pausing for a moment to stare around, before her steps turned to the door, a hand holding the side of her head.

Hand on the door, Imly stared at the lady who stood there, a frown etching across her face.

"I'm sorry. I think you have the wrong apartment." Imly started to close the door but paused as the lady shook her head.

"No, I'm in the right place. You're Imly Conroy. Darcie described you."

"I'm sorry. Darcie?"

The lady laughed. "Darcie Foster. A retired forensics psychologist and a good friend. She and her husband, Doug, a police lieutenant, were here this past week at the request of other friends. Let me introduce myself. I'm Rylee Allison, a friend of Emma and Abe, who I don't think you have met yet." With a grin on her face, she held up the box in her hands. "Darcie asked me to bring you some sweets."

Imly finally stood back, motioning for Rylee to enter. "I guess, the kitchen. I'm sorry, this is all so new. Brendon and I had not been married long when we were kidnapped." She reached for the kettle, but paused, fighting the tears she could not stop.

Rylee gave an inaudible sound and simply swept Imly into a hug. "It's hard. It's so hard. I know that." She finally maneuvered Imly to a seat, before she reached to wring out a cloth in warm water to hand to her. Then, with the kettle on, she searched for tea and the teapot, and then the sugar and cream.

Imly looked up, her eyes red from her tears. "I should be doing that."

"No, you're to rest. I met your Doc downstairs. He was adamant that I look after you." Rylee searched for cups and small plates, opening the box to display a selection of baked goods. "You wouldn't know, but I have a bakeshop. Darcie told me that you needed some sweets." Rylee sat, her eyes on Imly, before she reached for one of Imly's hand, her head bowing as she prayed.

"Dear Father, my new friend is hurting, in so many ways. I know some of the pain she feels, dear Lord. But it's not the same. Our pain is so individual, just like us. It's hard to see the good stuff in all this, Lord. That's when You need to shake us and remind us that You are the One we look to and offer our praise to. It is You, dear Lord, who cradles us in Your hands and shelters us. We can only praise You for that. We can't totally understand it, now can we, Lord?"

Imly stared at Rylee as she prayed, never having heard someone talk to God in such an open and honest way. Rylee, looking up, caught the surprised look on Imly's face and laughed.

"I'm sorry. It's how I talk to God. I was taught that prayer is not just for certain times. It should be a day-long conversation with my Abba Father."

Imly finally nodded, the surprise wearing off. "That is so true." She sighed. "I wish it was that easy. Brendon told me that when he would brew coffee, he would pray for someone."

"That's it. Exactly." Rylee watched as Imly nibbled at a cookie. "I'm so sorry about your parents, Imly. I think that is why Darcie wanted me to come and see you. My parents were murdered when I was young, leaving my paternal grandmother to raise me and my two brothers."

"Wow! Your brothers must have been young."

"They were, but we made it. Dave, my husband, is the love of my life. If we had not moved here from Ireland, I would not have met him."

"Ireland? Strange that you came from there. Barnabas sent two of the men over there to investigate.

I can't remember if he told me what they found. It was told around that my father was involved in crime, but it wasn't him at all." Imly's finger moved crumbs around on the table.

"They said the same about my father, but he wasn't involved, not at all. In fact, he was one of the ones who was trying to bring men to justice. They killed him because of that. But when Dave and I went through what we did, we were able to solve that with the help of detective friends and bring them to justice." Rylee paused speaking, staring across the kitchen. "I almost died, Imly. And if Darcie were to tell you Doug and her story, you would not believe it. It sounds like something from a novel. Doug is the ETF lieutenant. A rogue police chief wanted revenge on all the emergency services. He almost took out a large number of people in our town. He also shot Darcie. If another friend who is a paramedic had not been there, she would have died. And my Dave is a paramedic as well. He's been involved in so much that we can't even talk about."

"I get that, Rylee." Imly sat back, a hand rubbing at the side of her head. "I hate this, you know. I really do. I don't see what purpose God has in me ending up with a skull fracture and Brendon dead. Or my parents dead."

"Do you know for sure that Brendon is dead?" Rylee looked past Imly towards the hallway, hearing the door open quietly and then close, the sounds of shoes being removed and then equally quiet footsteps heading their way.

Breck, Brody, and Dave, Rylee's husband, appeared in the kitchen, moving quietly around the two ladies, to make coffee for themselves, before they were seated at the table, reaching into the box for some of the goodies.

Startled at the feeling of more people in her kitchen, Imly looked up, her face whitening for a moment. Dave watched her closely before he shared a look with Breck.

"Imly?" Breck's voice drew her eyes to him. "How are you? And don't say that you're fine, because we know you're not."

Imly stared at him, not used to being spoken to in such a blunt manner, before she shrugged.

"I really don't know, Breck. I have a horrible headache, I look like something that the cat dragged in, my parents are dead, Brendon is gone, likely dead." Her words paused as she frowned. "They showed me a picture, Breck. But there was something off about it. I can't put my finger on it."

Chapter 23

Breck nodded, his eyes on Brody for a moment, before he spoke.

"Talk to us, Imly. Tell us what you can remember. It doesn't have to make sense, if that's what is holding you back. Experience has taught me that sometimes it's what seems the least in an investigation or an event that could make or break the outcome."

Imly sighed, her head really beginning to hurt. "I can try, Breck, but I'm not thinking too clearly right now."

"We understand that, Imly." Brody spoke up. "Just start talking. If we need to clarify something with you, we can."

Imly finally nodded, pain showing in her eyes. "I think. I'm not sure of anything, Breck. Does that make sense?"

"It does. With your head injury, you may not remember exactly what happened. That we understand. Dallas is trying hard to track your steps but he can't seem to find anyone who saw you. Or at least, anyone who will acknowledge that."

"Wills has them scared. That much I know. He terrifies me, Breck. But I don't think that he was the one this time. I don't recall hearing his voice. It was someone different, someone I know but I can't remember who at the present." She reached for her cup, her hand shaking as she raised it to her mouth to sip from it, her other hand coming up to help steady it.

"Just take your time, Imly." Breck had reached for the pad of paper that he had set to one side, his pen in his hand. "I'll take notes and then we can go back over them."

"Old school, Breck? I didn't think anyone used pen and paper anymore."

Breck grinned as Brody laughed. "I do, Imly. I find I think better if I write it out this way. Okay. So, where do we start?"

"At the beginning, I guess." Imly frowned. "I know that person who was there. Quite well, I think, but I just don't know. I can't remember who it is." She sighed. "I have to go back, I think, to when it all started. We talked about it, right?"

"We did, Imly. You were upfront and honest with us. Wills had you kidnapped and brought down here. He had been stalking you, trying to date you. A man his age? He'd be in his fifties at least."

"He is. Fifty-five in fact. He made sure that I knew that. I hated him being around him. He made me feel dirty and unclean. I can't quite explain what I mean. I think I told you that my employer protected me as much as he could until I had to quit. This took a lot of my freedom away from me.

"When we arrived here, he was waiting in a house outside town. I had no freedom until one day I was able to escape, shoving him from me. He told me that we would be married that day. I couldn't stay here. I know he looked for me here in town. I made a few friends over the three or four days I was on the streets. They protected me. Not one of them liked Wills. He is linked to more crime that what you have discovered. One of them told me that he tried to recruit some of them to break into homes and businesses and steal artwork and jewelry, that he would then sell on the black market or ship overseas.

"Now, to come to the present. I think Wills was behind our abduction, but I can't say for sure. I always felt that there was someone else involved, someone who had power over him. He's a coward and a bully. I just don't know who." She paused, reaching for her tea, sipping it even though it had grown cold.

"To go back to when you had told us about a heritage you had coming to you. The fellows have confirmation that there is none. And that there has not been in years. The official they spoke with would not confirm if there was a criminal element still promoting that idea." Brody looked at Breck, finding him watching Imly closely.

Imly nodded, fatigue weighing her down. "I understand that. I just don't know why Dad would have told me that." She paused before she shook her head. "As to this kidnapping, I can't tell you much. I don't remember, excepts for bits and pieces that aren't clear. Except for that photo."

"What is striking you wrong about the photo?" Rylee spoke, her eyes on Dave as he nodded. They had faced something similar.

"I'm not sure." Imly turned to her. "It just didn't seem to be Brendon. The man's build was off. He was laying in such a way that I couldn't see his face." A cry came from her. "There was no wedding band. I could see his left hand. There was no wedding band. And Brendon had one." She held up her hand. "He bought me one to give him that matched mine. A rose gold one and engraved, which is unusual. Does that mean it wasn't him?"

"Quite possibly. They would have been playing mind games with you, Imly." Breck looked down at his notes. "You said there was blood on the chest?"

"There was, but there was no hole in his shirt." She paused once more. "And it wasn't the shirt Brendon had on. I doubt they would have made him change it. It was somewhat similar in colour, but it didn't match."

"Then, I think we can safely say, it was not likely Brendon who you saw. Whether that man is alive or dead, that we will have to leave to the police." Breck looked up, a thoughtful look on his face. "What else, Imly?"

"I don't know." She buried her face in her hands, her headache increasing. "I don't know. I seem to remember walking to the church. From the lake or thereabouts. Does that make sense?"

"It does. There is a direct road or several paths that come up to the church from there. We can start looking that way." Brody rose at a nod from Breck. "I'll go find some of the guys. We have time yet today that we can search."

Breck watched him walk away, the door closing quietly behind him, before he looked back to Imly, seeing how white and drained she had become.

"Imly, we'll leave it at this today. You do need to be resting."

"I know, Breck, but resting does not bring Brendon back." Her face whitened even more as a look of absolute horror crossed her face and a cry was wrenched from deep within her. "I know who it was."

———

Her eyes rolled back as she collapsed, sliding from her chair.

Dave had been on the move before she had spoken, catching her in his arms and then looking around.

"Down the hall, Dave. The last room on your left is the bedroom. I'll find Doc." Breck was out of his chair, heading for the main floor, knowing Doc would be there somewhere.

Rylee reached to pull the blankets back before Dave gently laid Imly in her bed, pulling them back up before she stood to one side, watching as Dave worked over Imly.

Chapter 24

Doc walked back through the apartment, a grave look on his face. He simply shook his head at Breck before he walked to the apartment door and through it, looking for Barnabas among their friends gathered there.

"Doc?" Brady approached, Barnabas beside him. "How is she?"

"We need to admit her, Brady. I am not convinced that there is not something going on. We need to do imaging and I may need to call in another specialist." He paused, not quite sure how to express what he needed to. He wasn't all that familiar with Imly, not enough to know how she would react if he said much about her condition.

"Doc? Are you thinking bleeding?" Barnabas shared a look with Brady, who nodded. That had been his thought.

"I am. It may be nothing, but I would rather err on the side of caution. Brady? Who's working today?"

"Tammy and Luke."

"Good. They'll take care of her. Request them when you call it in."

"Already done." He walked away, heading for the main entrance, to wait for his colleagues.

Barnabas watched him walk away before he spoke.

"How serious, Doc?"

"Now, that I can't tell you. Breck seemed to think that she had remembered something. He was grateful that God had placed Dave there today."

"It is how He works, isn't it?" Barnabas rubbed at his face. "Mom and Dad are heading this way, he said. They are concerned. He is not sure if he knows her parents."

"Then from who? Do either one of them have siblings?"

"Her father. And no one knows exactly where he is right now, not that I know of."

"I can tell you exactly where he is." Burnie spoke from beside him. "He's here in town. Dallas is back in town and has confirmed sightings of him."

"He does?" Doc shook his head. "Is he the one behind all this?"

"I would suspect so." Burnie shook the sheaf of papers in his head. "This is only part of what we have found. He was estranged from her father, had been for a number of years, but confirmation is coming that he was seen frequently in her home town and around their home."

"This has to hurt. Finding out this will set her back in her healing." Barnabas turned for a moment, his eyes on the door to the apartment. "Buckley called a bit ago. He's got the prayer chain working and has set up the room in the church and in the chapel here. He said there have been many calls, asking how the people can help."

"That's good." Doc paced away before he spun and returned. "Has she said anything at all?"

Breck spoke from behind him. "She's adamant now that the man in the photo was not Brendon, but just who it was, we don't know. Imly has been able to remember enough of what bothered her that convinced her that they were lying to her about the photo. But she is not convinced that Brendon is still alive. She thinks she walked to the church from the lake area. Some of the men have taken a look this afternoon but came back as soon as word reached them about her."

"She won't like that." Doc shook his head before his hand reached for the doorknob to the apartment door. "I'll be with her. We need to solve this, men, and soon."

They watched as Doc disappeared before turning to the others gathered around them, the men and their ladies, the single men, the teens. Barnabas drew a deep breath. Every time one of his friends went through something, it seemed to be worse. He had a dread of what the others would face, but he also acknowledged that God was in control.

Rylee met Doc as he paused in the kitchen, concern on her face.

"Doc? Imly is awake and is adamant that she will not go back to the hospital. Dave has checked her vitals, her vision, and said they are within normal limits."

Doc sighed. "We can't force her, but she'll be here on her own." Doc made a move to head for the bedroom when Rylee's hand stopped him.

"She knows that, Doc. She told us that she was fine with that, that if she needed someone she would call. She has expressed her desire to be on her own." Rylee was concerned, that was evident. "I can understand that, Doc. You don't know my history or Dave's. My parents were murdered when I was sixteen, leaving my younger brothers and me on our own except for Dad's mother. I know that feeling of wanting to be on my own, to grieve, to come to terms with what she has to face."

"But you weren't injured." Doc pointed past her. "She has a head injury. This episode today? It could be a bleed on the brain."

"It could, but we can't force her to treatment." Rylee watched with compassion as Doc's mouth worked as he tried to control his emotions. Imly had a way, with her soft voice and her demeanour of not wanting to make trouble for anyone, of wrapping herself into their heartstrings on first meeting.

"No, we can't." Doc sighed, turning as Brady tapped at the door and entered. "Brady, sent the crew away. Imly won't go."

Brady nodded. "Already did. We talked, the three of us. We figured this would be the situation." He shook his head in turn. "We'll watch for her."

"But not overnight. She is adamant that she won't have anyone around her. She doesn't want to put anyone out, as she stated it."

Brady stared at Rylee. "She said that? She doesn't know us. We won't let that happen."

"Unfortunately, Brady, we have to respect her wishes. I made sure all our numbers are on her phone." Doc walked away from them, heading towards Imly.

Dave had a few quiet words with Doc before he moved away, finding Rylee waiting for him.

"Dave?" Rylee walked into his hug.

"Imly won't budge." Dave sighed, knowing he would have done the same. "It's her choice."

"It is. A voice inside me says something is going to break loose soon. And she will be hurt once more."

Dave nodded, his hug tightening. "I know, love. I know. All we can do is pray for her."

Chapter 25

A week passed and then a second one. Imly wandered the apartment and then the building and then the outdoors, trailed when she did that by one of the security guards. She was now on a first-name basis with them all, she thought.

She had lain awake each night, finally rising around four to pace the apartment before she would find her Bible and spend the next hours in prayer and Bible study. She was growing in that way, coming more aware of God working in her life. She was trying hard to learn to praise in this situation, but it was tough, she acknowledged to the ladies, who would spend time with her each day, taking turns. They had agreed with her but told her that all she had to do was be willing. God knew her heart and how hard it was for her.

Imly also spent time in the conference room, as much as they would let her, reading through the material that she would find on the table in front of the chair she favoured. The men would study her and then look at one another, shaking their heads. They had each returned to their normal occupation, knowing that at some point, they would be called away again.

Brody had taken to spending his time seated next to Imly. He was concerned, monitoring the whiteness or grayness of her face, as the case may be. When he questioned how she was feeling, she would simply shrug and respond that she had no idea how she was to feel, that she had never been in such a situation before.

Imly frowned as she stared at the pages in front of her four weeks after she had returned home. Her strength was gradually returning, not because she has keeping up the diet Doc had given her. She was grateful for his loving care but it didn't make it any easier. She rubbed at her forehead, the headache still there but only a dull roar, was how she now termed it.

Looking up, she searched for someone who could help her understand what she was reading. It didn't make sense, but then in a bizarre way, it did. She had not told anyone who it was that she suspected of being behind Wills. She still had not come to terms with that.

"Imly? You look puzzled?" Brennen sat on one side of her, Branigan on the other.

"I am. This? These dates? Who came up with them?" Imly's finger tapped at the paper.

Branigan leaned over to read what had caused her concern. "Jace or Emma, I think. We didn't. I don't think that we've seen those. I don't remember them at all. Brennen?"

Brennen had reached for the paper, leafing through them. "No, this is new stuff. Emma has sent it. We Haven't had it given to us yet. How?"

Imly shrugged. "It was sitting here, where I usually sit. I thought one of you had put it there."

"No, I don't think that we did." Branigan was on his feet, his phone out, questioning each man before he returned. "Burnie did. He has copies for each of us, which we Haven't got yet. He said they're in a pile on the table." He looked around. "I don't see them."

———

125

"They're not here. That is strange. Who would have taken them?" Brennen was on his feet in turn, heading for the security guard.

"Does it matter?" Imly was puzzled at their reaction.

"It does, Imly. If someone has taken them, then either it was one of the security personnel or someone was in here, getting in through a locked door, and removing all the copies but that one." He reached for her copy. "May I borrow this for a few minutes? I want to make copies."

Imly shrugged. "Sure. Whatever."

Branigan was back in his chair, a stern look on his face. "That's not right, Imly. It is not "whatever". You matter to us. Whether you have accepted it or not, you are part of the Foundation family."

She sighed. "I know that. I just have trouble remembering that. For so many years, it was just my parents and me." She looked up at him. "What do we know about that?"

"The police are not saying. Nor is Dallas. He wants to meet with you sometime this week, I think."

"He said that. I'm not sure I'm ready to. Not without Brendon." Her voice was quiet enough that Branigan could barely hear her.

"We know, Imly. We know. Now, about this?" He was on his feet, heading for the photocopier, making his copies, and then back in his chair beside her, her copy in front of her. "Talk to me. Tell me what you see."

"What I see? I see dates that don't make sense. These dates for my parents' birthdays? That's not what we always celebrated. Mine is correct. Their anniversary is wrong." A thought crossed her mind. "Branigan, do you have photos that would go with these dates?"

His hand stilled from where he had been running his finger down the page, the other hand with his pen jotting notes. "I'm not sure. What are you thinking?"

"That may be the people who I believed were my parents, weren't. Is that a possibility?"

"That is what I need to talk to you about, Imly." Dallas' voice from beside her had her jumping in her chair even as she turned, a white look on her face.

"They weren't my parents, were they?"

"No, they weren't. I'm sorry, Imly. I truly am. They were the ones who were connected to Wills at some point. We also have evidence that they were connected to the criminal group in Ireland who noised around about that heritage you were to receive."

"Then, who am I?" Imly could barely whisper the words, tears near the surface.

"You are Imly MacDermott. That we have proven. We are working on finding your real parents, but have hit a roadblock there."

"How old would I have been when this happened?"

"We're not sure, but likely a baby or young toddler. You don't have any memories, do you?"

———

"Not of anyone but them. They loved me, Dallas. How could that be?" Imly rose, running from the room, unable to stem the tears, brushing past Ennis and Hagen as they called to her.

The two women stared after her and then at one another, before looking at Branigan, who had followed Imly from the room.

"Branigan?" Hagen turned to watch where Imly had fled to. "What just happened?"

"She just found out her parents were not her parents."

"What? Oh, my!" Ennis turned as well. "Someone needs to be with her."

"Let her be for now, Ennis. Check on her later." Branigan turned away from them, returning to the conference room, determination of his face to find out just who that couple was.

128

That night, the moon and stars were hidden behind the heavy dark clouds that dripped a cold misty rain on the ground. The wind was strong, blowing in from the lake, a bitter chill to it, sending the late autumn leaves scurrying to the ground in front of it. The man paused for a moment outside the Foundation building, searching for anyone that might see him, before he adjusted his hold on the second man, leading him to the back door. He reached for the keys in the man's jacket pocket and unlocked the door, letting him in and then handing him his keys. He waited as the man hesitated and then walked forward, his steps slow and weighted, his hand running along the wall to help balance himself.

Brendon slowing climbed the stairs to the third floor, each stair seeing higher than the one before it, needing to stop every few steps to catch his breath. He didn't know where the man was, who told him to call him John, that he would get him to safety. He needed his help to continue, only he was on his own.

Finally reaching his own door, he leaned against the wall, his face gray and drawn in the overhead lighting. He fumbled with his keys to unlock the door, stepping into the apartment, the door closing behind him, and reaching down to remove his shoes, out of habit setting them into the closet. He drew a deep breath as he straightened back up.

John had found him the day before, he thought, freeing him from his prison and taking him to safety. After four weeks, Brendon was grubby and unkempt, his hair long, his face covered in whiskers that he hated but hadn't been able to do anything about.

John had let him sleep, rousing him only to get broth and water down his throat. He had watched Brendon carefully, his skills as an armed forces medic coming into play. Brendon had roused about three hours previously, a question on his lips that never was asked. John had helped him into the shower, Brendon shaky on his feet, leaving clean clothes for him, before he had seated him at a table, and without waiting for Brendon to refuse, played barber for the younger man.

Brendon, once more clean-shaven and with his hair trimmed neatly, had gratefully eaten the soup placed before him, too tired to even ask who John was and how he had found him. He had paid little attention as John had walked him from the lake area to the Foundation building, not even questioning how John knew where he belonged.

He walked slowly through his apartment, a frown puckering his forehead, as he saw the dim light from his bedroom. That is strange, he thought. I don't remember leaving a light on. He stared down at the wedding band on his finger, his thoughts on his bride. Lord, they told me she was gone, but they wouldn't tell me if she had left me or if she was dead. That played on my mind. It was so hard to try and praise You in those circumstances. I tried, Lord, I really did.

Making his way through his apartment to the bedroom, Brendon rifled in his dresser for his nightclothes, heading for the ensuite bathroom to change, before he headed towards the bed. His steps slowed and then stopped. Wonder lit his face as he saw Imly, asleep, her hand on his pillow, traces of the tears that she had wept in her sleep on her face.

She is here, Lord. I didn't know that. I wonder if John did. Thank you, Lord, that she is here and alive. He slipped in beside her, his arms coming out to wrap around her and cradle her to him. His own tears wet the red hair that he loved, even as he slipped away to sleep, his body unable to keep him alert or awake.

Awakening in the early morning hours, as had become her custom, Imly lay, her eyes closed, sensing something different around her. She slowly opened her eyes, a frown on her face as she realized she was held firmly in someone's arms. Momentary fear drove through her until she raised her head and saw Brendon. Her own wonder grew before she raised herself even more, to drop a kiss on his cheek, before she slipped away, to dress and then head for the kitchen.

I will let him sleep, won't I, Lord? I have no idea where he came from or when, but I am thankful that he is here with me. Time enough to talk later today. She hummed a praise chorus without realizing that she was, as she fixed her tea and then set the coffeemaker, ready to turn it on when Brendon awoke. She paused, her hand resting on the fridge door, her eyes turning towards the hallway, listening for Brendon's movements.

Imly reached for her phone, to check her messages as had become her habit on a daily basis. She smiled. Breck had sent his usual good morning message. He had taken on the role of a big brother to her, one that she desperately had needed. She scrolled through the messages, tears briefly blinding her as she read them. Each one of the fellows, including Barnabas, had sent messages of encouragement for her. The ladies had each sent a thought or a prayer or a Bible verse for her. She hadn't realized just how they

131

had taken her into their growing family, but today, she finally understood.

Lost in thought, she had not heard Brendon moving around in the bedroom or the soft sounds of his footsteps as he padded towards the kitchen. Brendon paused in the doorway, his eyes on her, thankful once more that she was alive and that he was home with her. Now, he thought, we need to find out who is responsible for the destruction and devastation that they had both undergone.

He walked towards her, his arms coming around her, causing a small squeak to come from her, before she wrapped her arms around him.

"When did you get home, Brendon?" Her voice was muffled against him.

He shrugged. "I'm not sure. I wasn't too awake last night or rather early this morning. Somewhere around one, I think. John didn't tell me."

"John? Who's that?" Imly was puzzled. She didn't know a John, or at least, she didn't think she did.

"He's the one who found me, fed me, cleaned me up, and brought me back to you." Brendon's arms tightened around her. "They told me that you were gone. I just didn't know if you had left me or were dead."

Imly shuddered at her own memories. "They told me that you were dead. They even showed me a picture, but we've figured out that it wasn't you. We just don't know who it was."

"No? Maybe I can help." He swayed slightly, fatigue hitting him unawares. He reached for a chair to sit, Imly's hand resting on his shoulder. "Imly? Are

———

you okay?" He searched her face, seeing that she had been through a trial without him.

"I'm getting there, my love. I was hurt. I escaped from Wills but fell somehow. I'm not even sure how now. Anyway, I hit my head hard enough to fracture the skull." She watched as his eyes slid closed before she wrapped her arms around him once more. "I made it to the church and Buckley got me to help. I'm better every day."

"Oh, sweetheart, I wish I had been there. They have taken so much time from us."

"That they have." Imly moved away, to switch on the coffeemaker before she turned back to him. "We are researching and investigating. Someone named Emma is sending information to us and to Dallas."

"Emma? That's good. She finds things no one else can, but can't explain how she does it."

Imly looked towards the outside door as a tap came to it. "That will be one of the fellows or one of the ladies. They have made it a habit of appearing each morning, just to make sure I'm okay."

"They're a great bunch." Brendon took the mug of coffee she handed him before he reached to kiss her, not wanting her to move from his sight, his arm around her waist to keep her near him.

"Brendon. I need to answer the door." Imly shook her head at him even as she smiled, content for the moment.

"I know." He sighed. "I guess that means it will get out that I'm home."

"It will. You don't know how worried all of them have been." Imly moved away from him, to open the door.

Doc stood there, as well as Dave and Rylee, his mouth open to speak before he snapped it closed.

"When did he get home?" Rylee's soft question came even as she hugged Imly.

"Sometime last night. I didn't hear him at all." Imly looked up at Doc. "He's not in great shape, Doc. He said someone named John found him and brought him home."

Chapter 27

Shaking his head, Doc stepped away from Brendon, who was seated in his office chair. He was not sure what all Brendon had been through, but he seemed to be in good health, and that Doc could not understand. The wound from the bullet had healed well, Doc was glad to see.

"Brendon? What can you tell us?" Dallas spoke from where he was perched on the corner of the desk. He had appeared just after Doc had entered their apartment.

"I'm not sure what all I can tell you. I never saw the faces on the men, and there were only two that came around me. I was locked into some sort of hole in the ground, with a door to go in and out. I could see the sky above and yes, it did rain down on me. It was not a pleasant place to be." He shook his head. "I didn't really see them much. I slept a lot, I think, and when I would be asleep, that seems to be when the food and water that they provided appeared in my cage. They would come around, ask me questions that didn't make sense and then disappear."

Dallas looked up from his notes. "What sort of questions?"

Brendon shrugged. "Just about who I was, where I was from, who my parents were. I didn't answer, and they didn't like that. About two weeks ago, they told me that Imly was gone, but refused to clarify that. I didn't know if she had left me or was dead."

"And that played with your mind." Dallas stared at him for a moment, before his eyes dropped to his notes. "Now, you mentioned a John. Who is he?"

Brendon shook his head. "I have no idea who he is. He just appeared, not yesterday, the day before, opened the door, dragged me to my feet, and led me from there. I couldn't tell you where we ended up. I just couldn't concentrate. He fed me, let me sleep, helped me to clean up, and then brought me here. He didn't say a word the whole time. And I can't remember what he looked like."

Dallas nodded. Brendon's comment was about what he expected him to say. "How about the men that held you captive?"

Brendon shrugged, not willing to say. "Average height. Average weight. Neatly kept. One had blond hair, one brown. Clean-shaven. I really wasn't paying that much attention." He sighed. "And no, I won't work with a police artist. I don't remember enough to describe them. Besides, it was dim, with only the light coming from the hole above me."

"Okay." Dallas shared a look with Doc and then Dave, who was closely watching Brendon.

Dave mentally shook his head. He knows more, doesn't he, Lord? He's just not saying. They must have threatened Imly, that would be the only reason that he won't say.

Doc and Dallas finally walked away, Dave's head turning to watch them, before he looked over at Brody and Brennen, who were seated nearby, their eyes on Brendon.

"What didn't you tell him, Brendon?" Dave's voice was quiet.

"What do you mean?" Brendon wasn't sure about Dave, only having met him that morning, although Imly seemed to trust him.

"You know more than you said. Or you suspect more than what you told him." Dave leaned forward, reaching for the pad of paper and pen laying on the desktop.

Brendon sighed. "You're right. What I couldn't say are impressions that I had." He looked over at Brody. "You two know me. I don't make accusations."

"No, you don't, but you have an impression that you can't shake." Brennen looked towards the doorway. "Right now, Brendon, I would say that you need to rest. Doc's heading back this way, and I think you'll find Imly with him."

Imly appeared in the doorway, a frown on her face at Brennen's words. "Brennen?"

"It's okay. We're just trying to get Brendon to take it easy."

"I know. Brendon, Lawrence is here. He's asking about you."

Brendon gave a slow nod and started to stand. Lawrence had appeared behind Imly, and then moved past her, motioning Brendon to stay seated before he seated himself in front of the desk, nodding at the other three men and motioning Imly to stay.

"Brendon? What did Doc have to say?" Lawrence was concerned, more about Brendon's health than that he was behind in his orders in the shop.

"That I need to rest. I want to come back, Lawrence, even part-time. Is that possible?" Brendon knew that he was pushing it.

"You can. Edward has stepped in for now, but he's not interested in full-time work. His work with the teens is where his heart is."

"I know. This is Thursday. How be I start part-time again on Monday?" He looked up at Imly, who was standing beside him, her hand on his shoulder, his arm around her waist. "And Imly will come with me. She's eager to take over in the office."

Lawrence's face lit up. "You are?" At Imly's nod, his smile grew bigger. "That is an answer to prayer. With you in the office, I can go back into the workshop."

"But, Lawrence, what if I bring danger or trouble to your business?" Imly had considered that many times while Brendon was missing.

"I thought of that. Barnabas has been in touch. He sent a security guard over to assess what I need and I have made the changes he suggested. No one gets into the workshop or office area. We have a locked steel door. The showroom has been redesigned to some degree, with more of the items showcasing on the website. We'll make it work, Imly."

Lawrence finally left, Brendon secretly glad that he had. He was exhausted but he just couldn't rest, not until he talked to his friends. It looked as if Dave was now a friend as well.

"Dave? What do you do?" Brendon was searching for answers to questions he didn't know how to ask.

———

"I'm a paramedic. I'm friends with Doug and Darcie. And Abe and his men. Abe, Doug, and I grew up together. And if you need more information from a security standpoint, talk to Abe. I'm sure Barnabas already has."

"He has." Brody spoke up. "But for now, we're not doing anything more. Brendon, your volunteer work with the badminton club has been taken care of. Burnie was glad to step in. He states that he needs some new ideas for his novels and this is a perfect opportunity to try and find some."

Brendon grinned, his mind eased on that front. "He does, does he? I'm sure the teens will give him plenty of that."

Dave was finally the only one left in the room with Brendon, the two friends leaving to head to their employment, and Imly had left with Rylee to find some of the ladies in the building. Dave studied Brendon closer, seeing the fatigue, but also something else.

"What else is bothering you, Brendon?"

Brendon looked up, surprised at the question. "I'm not sure what you mean."

"I mean, there is something else, something that you Haven't told anyone else. And before you deny it, I've been there. Rylee and I went through some pretty intense stuff around the time we got married. I almost lost her. So, I do have a sense of what you are feeling."

"You did?" Brendon drew in a breath. "Yes, there is something. Imly said her parents are dead, that they have been identified, but that it has been proven that they were not her biological parents. I don't see that. How do we prove or disprove that?"

Chapter 28

Nodding, Dave leaned back in his chair, a thoughtful look on his face. He finally looked up at Brendon, finding the other man watching him closely.

"You have doubts? How were they identified?"

"Imly said it was the police in her hometown. I don't trust some of them. One of them had connections to the man, Wills, who had her kidnapped and brought down here. And then, there's John. How does he fit in? He never said anything. I have no idea who he is or where he is even from, or how he even found me."

"I can have Emma or Jace look into him. If you can describe him, that is."

"I can only in a vague sort of way. My mind was so fogged with a lack of sleep and nutrition. I am not sure that I wasn't drugged at some point."

"You more than likely were. You have no idea where you were?"

Brendon shook his head. "I don't. So, how do we prove that it was them? And how do we prove that they were or were not her parents?"

"Let Emma work on that. And a friend's wife can as well. She has a family tree program that she will gladly use. Just let me have all the information you can on Imly's family."

Later that afternoon, Imly found Brendon still seated at his desk, his computer up, his cold mug of coffee on the desk beside him. She simply shook her head, removed the mug, and headed for the kitchen to make him fresh. She paused as she did so, a thought niggling at her mind, before she shook her head. No, she didn't think that she knew the man Brendon called John, but when he had described what he could remember, he seemed familiar.

Having spent a number of hours in the conference room with the men and the ladies, Imly was exhausted, her headache returning. She had overdone it, she knew, but she was pushing herself to solve this mystery surrounding herself. It was only when it was solved and the culprits in custody that she felt Brendon and she could go on with their lives.

Brendon finally looked up, rubbing at his eyes, squinting towards the window. He was shocked to see that dusk had fallen. His eyes dropped to his work. He had made progress, he thought, but just what that was, he wasn't quite sure. Brendon knew he would need to talk with his friends, to get their perspective on what he had found and to see how it all correlated with what they were working on.

He rose, searching the apartment for Imly, standing beside the bed where he found her curled up, her arms wrapped around her, a gray look on her face. His finger reached to gently trace the track of her tears. Brendon sighed. He wanted to make it all better for her, but just couldn't. Lord, why? Why Imly? How do we praise You in these circumstances? This is taking a toll on her, on her body, on her mind, on her spirit.

Brendon reached for the blanket that Imly had folded neatly at the end of the bed and tucked it around her, a hand resting gently on her head as he prayed for his bride. He turned finally, heading for the kitchen, a glance at the clock showing it was past their supper time. He wasn't hungry but knew he needed to eat.

An hour later, Brendon stood in the conference room, facing Baird, Benen, and Blair, who were grouped in a half-circle in front of him. He could see the other men watching closely, all but Barnabas, and he knew that Barnabas had a meeting that he had to be out of town.

"What are you saying, Baird?" Brendon shook his head, not quite comprehending what he had been told.

"That Imly's parents are not dead. The couple that they found? They looked similar to them, but Barnabas asked that DNA testing be done. Dallas called, looking for either one of you. He asked that I tell you or Imly that her parents are still alive. We just don't know where they are."

Brendon's eyes slid shut, his emotions getting the best of him for a moment. "So, they are alive? How do we find them?"

Baird shook his head. "That we don't know. No one has seen them since that day Imly spoke with them. Emma's working on that, but she had a rush investigation that she had to take on. She apologized but said she'd be working on it again as soon as she could."

Brendon felt a hand on his back and reached to wrap an arm around Imly. "Imly? I thought you were sleeping."

"I was." Imly still had the gray, drawn look on her face, and the pain from her headache showed in her eyes. "My parents are still alive? Is that what you just said?"

"They are." Baird shared a look with Benen and Blair. "We just don't know where they are at present."

Imly nodded, a hand resting on the side of her head. "I have no idea where they would be. Unless Wills has them in his control and has hidden them somewhere." She paused. "Brendon, this John? Can you describe him again?"

Brendon proceeded to do so, his eyes on Imly as she frowned and then turned, breaking away from him to head for a computer, seating herself. He watched as her head bowed for a moment before he was in the chair beside her, an arm around her, Breck moving in on her other side, the other men gathering around.

"Imly? Sweetheart?"

Imly looked up, a clear look in her eyes again. "I think I might know him. You said he seemed to know how to treat you medically?"

"That was my impression. His care went beyond just an ordinary person."

Brady spoke up. "In other words, he assessed you and went from there in how he treated you?" At Brendon's nod, Brady continued. "Then, he's either in the medical field, has had training, or is retired from some sort of service or healthcare company."

"Then, I think that I do know him." Imly's fingers flew across the keyboard as she searched for a name, finally pulling up a news story. "Is this him, Brendon?"

Brendon stared at the photo on the screen, before he swallowed hard and then nodded. "It is. How?"

"I Haven't seen him in years. He's Dad's brother, but we Haven't seen in him something like five years. No, more like ten. He was in the armed forces, serving as a medic. He retired, suffering from post-traumatic stress disorder. He hadn't really remained in one place for too long." She looked up. "But, how did he end up here? And to find you?"

"That's something we will ask him when we find him. And find him we will." Brendon's arm tightened on her. "I guarantee you, we will find him."

Chapter 29

Lawrence turned from where he had been sanding a table and watching Brendon closely. Brendon had been back to work for almost two weeks, not saying a lot about what had happened to him, but that was alright with Lawrence. He knew Brendon kept a lot inside but would talk to him if he felt he needed to. His eyes turned to where the office was, and a smile crossed his face. He could hear Imly singing to herself, and he nodded. She had made a difference in his workload, taking on the office work.

Brendon paused his staining, staring at the dresser he had just finished, before he tapped the lid back on the can of stain and walked over to the large stainless steel sink that they used for cleaning their equipment, setting the brush into the container of paint thinner to clean. He shook his head. They were no further ahead, he thought, than they had been.

Imly thoughtfully replaced the phone receiver. Whoever it had been really didn't want to order furniture, now did they, she thought. A fishing expedition was more like it. She had not taken the bait, simply keeping her comments on the products that Lawrence carried or could manufacture. She rose from her desk, stretching, her eyes on the monitor for the security camera at the front of the store. He's back, isn't he? She almost ran from the office, searching for Brendon, throwing herself at him as she shook with terror.

Lawrence took one look at her and ran for the office, his eyes on the monitor as well even as he reached for the phone to call for help.

Brendon hugged her tight, his chin resting on the top of her head, feeling her shaking in her fear.

"Is he out there, love?"

"He is, pacing around the front of the building. What did I do, Brendon? I've brought trouble to Lawrence."

"No, you Haven't, Imly." Lawrence spoke from behind her. "I know that man, but not by the name you call him. He's tried to weasel his way into part ownership of the shop. I won't have him on the premises. Stay back here, you two. I called for the police to come and I was assured there was a patrol car in the area. Hopefully, they will be able to arrest him and keep him in jail for a while."

"Not long enough, Lawrence." Imly shifted in Brendon's arms, turning to face him. "He'll make bail and be out in no time."

"I don't think so, love. When I spoke with Dallas last, they were looking for him. Apparently, he has been involved in incidents in other jurisdictions as Dallas put it. The charges against him include murder and extortion."

Imly relaxed back against him. "Does that mean he won't be around?" Her voice was barely audible.

"He won't, but someone else will be. That is guaranteed." Dallas spoke from where he had come to a halt beside Lawrence. "We know he's not working on his own. We also know there is someone over him. That person is staying well hidden."

Imly nodded, not liking what Dallas had to say. It had just confirmed what she thought.

"So, now what? I'm not staying hidden away for weeks or months. I can't live like that. Nor can Brendon."

"We realize that, Imly, and are trying to investigate, but we keep hitting a blank wall. And that we can't understand."

"That's because you're not looking in the right places. I told you about that officer in my hometown. I am sure, if you look hard enough, you'll find someone on your own force, near to the investigation that is stonewalling you." Imly broke away from Brendon and headed back to the office, her hand reaching for the phone receiver to answer an incoming call.

Brendon watched her walk away before he spoke.

"Dallas? Had you thought of that?"

Dallas sighed. "We have. We are investigating a few of our officers. We're not liking what we're finding. Will is speaking with their supervisors today. Unfortunately, we're not confident that we have found the one or ones that we need to."

"Find them and find them soon. If you don't, I'll do the looking. I don't want this to drag on. She's stressed and that's stressing me. It's not helping her heal. And she's missing her parents. Do you know where they are?" Brendon walked away, heading towards Imly, to find her with her head pillowed on the arms she had folded on the desk, her body shaking with her subdued sobs. He dropped to his knees beside her, gathering her close, his lips moving in prayer for her.

———

"Dallas?" Lawrence didn't ask anything more.

"I know, Lawrence. I know. It's been the same for all of them, hasn't it?"

"It has, but something about Imly makes me want to help her. And it's not just because she's part of the family. It's her."

"I know what you mean. She's the little sister everyone wants to have and doesn't have. That makes us protective of her." Dallas blew out a breath before he shook his head and then walked away,

Early that same evening, Brendon stood in the conference room, staring at the whiteboards on the walls, noting the new information written on them. He walked towards one, a finger tracing the name.

"Who is this?"

Branigan looked over his shoulder. "Dwayne Easton? He is a son of Wills. No one seemed to know that here in town. He's involved in the shady side of life in town."

"How deep?"

"About as deep as you can get." Brandon shoved a photo at him. "This is him."

Brendon stared down at it. "He's one of them."

"One of who?"

"The two men that held me." Brendon's finger tapped the photo. "He's the blond. Now, who's the one with the brown hair?"

Bradon's hand reached into his line of sight, to drop a photo on top of the one Brendon was still holding. "Here. This is a cousin of his. They're always seen together."

"And this is the other one. Do we know where they are?"

"We do. They're up in Imly's hometown, sitting in jail at present. They were arrested for break and enter at her home up there."

Chapter 30

Berneen and Cadee watched Imly walk towards them a few days later. They had agreed to meet for lunch, Imly not sure if she should put the ladies at risk. They had laughed at her, telling her that all the younger ladies in the building family had faced things and came through victorious. She would be no different.

Imly hesitated as she approached them, her eyes tracing past them, a frown on her face as she saw the man watching her before he turned and walked away. That was John, she thought. But why was he here? He obviously didn't want her to acknowledge him.

Berneen had watched Imly closely before she turned, her own eyes following the man walking away, making a mental note to take to Baird that night.

"Imly? Ready for some lunch?" Cadee grinned at her, pointing towards the restaurant near Lawrence's building.

"I am. This is a restaurant?" Imly looked up in awe at the round building. "I thought it was a tower of some kind."

"Not at all. The owners wanted to build a castle but weren't allowed by the town council. They compromised on just a tower. They call it The Turret."

"Interesting name. British food?"

Berneen laughed as she waved at one of the owners and then pointed to a table near the back of the restaurant. "Not at all. Canadian is the predominant choice. But they do have a wonderful fish and chips or fries or whatever you want to call them."

An hour later, Imly waved goodbye to the two and walked back towards the shop, her thoughts not on the lunch, but on the man that she had seen. Was that really John? She would likely never know for sure. Her steps slowed as she neared the back door, her hand reaching to key in the code before she slipped through the open door, closing it tightly behind her.

Frowning, Imly looked around. Brendon and Lawrence should be here at work but she could not hear anything. She searched, not finding either one, before she hurried to the office, her eyes on the monitor to the shop. She drew in her breath sharply before reaching for the phone.

Brendon and Lawrence stood side by side, just inside the showroom, in front of the shop door, their hands raised, their eyes on the man in front of them. No, Brendon thought, it isn't Wills, but he has to be connected to him in some way.

Lawrence shifted his weight slightly, his eyes on the windows behind the man, seeing the police officers approaching quietly. He nodded to himself. Imly must have returned and found us.

"What is it exactly that you want?" Brendon's voice held a touch of anger and also fear. He didn't want the man to know where Imly was.

"Your woman. That's who. She needs to come with me." The man pointed to the door. "She's back there. How be we go on back there and you find her for me?"

———

151

"Not happening." Brendon shook his head. "I just can't do that." His head turned for a moment as he heard a sound, leaving the other man an opportunity to raise the piece of wood he held and bring it down heavily on Brendon's head. Brendon collapsed, not a sound coming from him, as Lawrence watched in horror.

Imly's hands covered her mouth, containing the scream that she had almost released. Please, Lord, don't let him be hurt. I can't stand it if he is. She reached for her phone as it danced on the desk from the vibrations shaking it.

"Hello?" Her voice was hesitant, relief coming to her as she recognized Dallas' voice.

"Imly? Where are you?"

"In the office. Please? He just struck Brendon. Please?"

"We're outside, Imly. Officers will be going in the front. I need you to come to the back door. I'm right out there."

Imly ran for the door, hesitating for a moment, before she cracked it open, to find Dallas and officers waiting for her. He swept her from the building even as the officers entered, rushing her to his vehicle and shoving her inside it, to stand with his back to it, his eyes searching the surrounding area.

Imly watched as the man was finally led from the building and then paramedics moved in, Brady one of them. How does that happen, Lord? He's there whenever we need him, isn't he? That has to be Your hand.

Dallas moved away from the door, opening it before he crouched down, his eyes on her.

———

"Dallas?"

"Brendon's on his feet. He's refusing to go to the hospital. He's desperate to find you. They were told that you had been kidnapped and that he had to go with them."

Imly stared at him. "I saw that man, the one who I think helped Brendon. He was watching out for me when I met Berneen and Cadee. I think he is my Dad's brother. We Haven't seen him in years."

Dallas nodded, his eyes following the man walking towards them. "Here's Brendon. Brady's with him."

Imly almost shoved Dallas out of the way. She ran towards Brendon but never made it. She stumbled and fell, to lay still. Brendon stopped his forward walk, stunned, even as Brady pushed past him, to drop to his knees, a hand on Imly's back, shocked to see the blood spreading across her mid-back, before his hand was on his radio, calling for his partner to hurry.

Brendon's knees hit the pavement hard, sending a shock wave through his body, even as horror grew on his face.

"Brady?"

"She's been shot, Brendon." Brady glanced up quickly and then past him to where his partner, Patrick, was running towards him, the other team of paramedics on his heels.

"Shot?" Brendon's hand reached to touch her red hair, tears suddenly blinding him. "How?"

Dallas stood behind him, a hand on his shoulder, even as he spat out orders to the officers, who scattered.

———

153

Hours later, Brendon raised his eyes, a haggard look on his face, expecting to see the surgeon in front of him. They had rushed Imly into the Emergency Department and then to surgery. He frowned, staring at the man who had stopped in front of him.

"Brendon? Imly?"

Brendon shook his head. "I'm sorry. It's John?"

"I am. I just heard. Imly?"

Brendon pointed to the chair beside him. "Sit. I have no idea how much longer it will be." He scrubbed at his face with the heels of his hand, suddenly overly tired. "She's in surgery."

"Surgery? I heard on the street that she was hurt. I didn't know it was that bad." John's eyes were raised as he saw the men from the building gathering around them, the ladies keeping back, Anna among them.

"Yeah, well, it is. They've had her in surgery for over two hours. They were sure what all they would find when they went in, the surgeon said." Brendon slumped back, a devastated look crossing his face. "Why?"

"Why?"

"Yea, why?" Brendon looked up as Buckley sat beside him. "Buckley?"

"I don't have that answer for you, Brendon. I wish that I did." His heart hurt for his friends.

John shared a look with Buckley before he looked up at Barnabas, who waited beside him. He stood, a hand out to shake the other man's hand. "Barnabas Carey. I'm Imly's uncle. John Dickerson."

"That's who we thought you were. First, thank you for rescuing Brendon. Now, talk to us. And make sure it's the truth you tell us." Barnabas nodded his head towards the men surrounding them. "They won't take it lightly if you don't."

Brendon was on his feet, shoving his way past them, leaving them to stare after him, before Buckley was moving after him, to stand beside him as the surgeon met him.

"Doctor?" Brendon was almost afraid to ask.

"Brendon? It went better than I hoped." The surgeon's hand reached to catch his arm, to steady him on his feet. "I stayed with her through the recovery process. That's why it's been so long. The nurse said she had been out to see you."

Brendon nodded. "She has been. How is my wife?"

"She's in ICU for now but if it goes as I suspect, she'll be moved to the surgical floor tomorrow. Come, walk with me." He nodded as Buckley walked with them. "God was with her, Brendon. I hope you know that."

"I do, Doctor. I do. But what aren't you saying?"

"That it could have been much worse. The bullet missed the organs. It did nick an artery, but the quick work on the part of the paramedics helped her to survive."

"It did?" Brendon's steps slowed before he walked forward again. "Can I see her?"

"You can. For a while. And then we'll ask you to leave. There is an officer outside her door. Dallas placed him there." The physician stopped Brendon. "She will need time to recover. With the head injury she had a while ago, we need to watch her closely."

"The head injury? Does that factor in?" Buckley was watching Brendon, knowing that he really wasn't listening anymore.

"It could. We had to be careful what we gave her in the operating room and what we can give her for pain medications. I understand she's still be having headaches?"

"She has. She doesn't say much, but she does." Brendon walked away from the two men, heading for Imly, to stand beside her bed, a hand on her cheek, the other hand on hers. He finally lifted his eyes to study the monitors, before he looked back down at her.

Buckley watched him walk away. "He's hurting, James."

"He is. We've been praying for them, but it just doesn't seem to end, now does it?"

John had watched Brendon and Buckley walk away before he spoke.

"Any word on her parents?"

"Why would you ask that?" Breck had moved to stand beside John, not sure about him.

"I know they're missing." He shot Breck a look before he pulled out his wallet. "This needs to be kept quiet. I work for an organization that tracks people like Wills. That's how we knew about Brendon. It just took me some time to find him. Did you know he was only about a mile from the building?"

"A mile?" Breck shook his head. "Now, why would you say that?"

"Because it's the truth. Wills has control of a property that borders the Foundation land. It's buried deep in numbered companies and phony names." He looked up as Bradon moved closer. "I have all the information that your detective will need." John handed over a thick envelope to Barnabas. "There are copies in there for you as well and my contact information. I need to leave." He was gone before any of the men could stop him

Breck stared after him. "Did that just happen?"

"It did." Bradon was frustrated. "Now, how do we find him?"

"He'll find us, I suspect." Burnie poked at the envelope. "We need to take that back to the conference room."

"And we will, once we know how Imly is." Barnabas handed Breck the envelope and walked away, his phone out as he took a call.

Chapter 32

Four days later, as Breck parked in front of the Foundation building, he smiled grimly to himself. He had watched in the rearview mirror as the car following him had been pulled over by a patrol car. Dallas was taking no chances, that he knew. He shifted in his seat to peer back at Brendon.

Brendon roused from his thoughts, his arm tight around Imly.

"We're home?" He was surprised. He didn't realize that they had arrived there.

"We are. Let's get Imly inside." Breck slipped around to the back door to open it for Brendon, watching as Brendon stepped down from the truck, then reached to gather a sleeping Imly tight into his arms, a soft sigh coming from her as he did so.

Hagen waited to hold the building door open for them before she headed for the elevator, intent on helping. Breck had waved as he returned to his truck, to head back into town to a meeting.

Brendon gently laid Imly down on the bed, a murmur of thanks to Hagen before she moved away. He knelt beside it, his hand on his bride, his heart lifting in prayer. It could have been so much worse, he thought. He could have lost her and he didn't know how he would have ever lived on if he had.

He finally rose, tucked the blanket around her, and then headed for the kitchen, the aroma of freshly-brewed coffee heading down the hall to meet him. He reached for a mug, poured his cup, and then stood, staring at the fridge.

Hagen watched from where she stood near the sink, a slight smile on her face.

"Brendon?" When he looked around, she continued. "How is she? Really?"

"Lucky to be alive. James told me today that they almost lost her a couple of times during the operation. That's why he stayed in the recovery room with her, not just leaving the surgical assistant to do that." He sighed, reaching to pull a chair out from the table so he could sit, weary beyond what he had been. "God was good, Hagen. He was good. It is hard to praise Him at times, but I have no choice."

Hagen nodded as she took her own glass of water and sat with him, a hand rubbing at her abdomen. Brendon frowned at her as she laughed.

"It's okay, Brendon. I'm fine. The twins are kicking up a storm today. That's all." Hagen and Brandon were expecting twins, the first little ones in the building, and everyone was eagerly anticipating meeting them.

Brendon smiled. "They will be spoiled, you do know that? With all us in the building, how could it be anything else?"

Hagen laughed. "Haley and Hollie say the same thing. They drive me to distraction at times. They want to know if the babies are boys or girls. We chose not to find out." She looked closer at him. "You need to rest, Brendon. Working the hours you have as well as being at the hospital as much as you have been is wearing you down."

Brendon sighed. "I know. I just couldn't do anything else."

"We get that, Brendon. For now, one of the guys will drive you back and forth to work. Dallas and Barnabas have worked out a schedule. There will also be an officer in plain clothes in the building with you. From what I understand, the one who will be there is eager to learn the furniture trade. He's wanting to move on to something different, he tells Barnabas. He retires in four months and says he too young to sit around."

"Lawrence said that he had someone in mind. With the way the business is growing, even given the times we're living in, he wants to hire someone. He's spending more time designing that he really can afford to right now." He sighed once more. "But I don't want to leave Imly on her own."

"We understand that." Hagen picked up the sheet of paper that she had laid on the table and waved it at him. "The ladies have gotten together and drawn up a schedule, including Anna and Amy and the two teens. Darbie wants to help out with you. We are splitting the hours that you will be away among us, making sure for the first few days that she is not on her own. She'll grow tired of us."

Brendon paused as he raised his mug to his mouth and then shook his head. "No, I don't think so. She told me this morning that she finally had realized just how much she was a part of this family, that she felt wanted for the first time in years."

"She did? She is a part of us. But for years? What did she mean?"

"That I am not sure. She was asleep again before I could ask. Her uncle has been around when I've been there on my own. He's done some talking. I need to let the others know what he has been saying." He yawned and then apologized.

Hagen merely shook her head at him. "They're in the conference room. Head on down there, if you like. I can stay. Brandon expects you to come there."

Brendon finally stood, reached to hug his friend's wife, and then headed to check on Imly, finding her still sleeping, not having moved from the position he had left her in, before he headed down to the main floor. He paused outside the conference room door, hearing laughter coming through it as someone was being teased. His heart eased some in its sorrow, knowing that his friends were there for him, just as he was for them.

———

Chapter 33

Staring at the chart on the wall, Brendon was puzzled. He moved to stare at the map next to it, a finger coming up to trace the highway from Imly's hometown to where he lived. Somewhere along there, he felt her parents were. Whether they were free and on their own, or held captive to get to Imly, that he wasn't sure of.

Brody moved in beside him, Bradon on his other side, exchanging a glance behind his back.

"What are your thoughts, Brendon?"

Brendon's finger stabbed at a name. "John mentioned this village. He seemed to think that Ian had contacts there. How he knows that, I am not sure."

Bradon tilted his head. "That name did come up, but I can't remember why. Do you, Brody?"

"It was one of the ones the guys stopped at. They mentioned that the people were hesitant to talk to them, almost as if they were afraid." Brody shook his head. "One of us needs to head back there. It's only about forty-five minutes from here."

"That close and yet so far." Brendon paused. "If it wasn't that Imly was just home from the hospital, I would head there. Tomorrow's Saturday."

"Devaney's scheduled to be with her tomorrow, Brendon, even though you're home. The ladies want to take some of the burdens from you. This is how they feel they can serve you two. They don't want to step on your toes and will back away if either of you wants them to.”

Brendon shook his head. “No, it’s fine. I know that they care deeply for Imly. She told me she’s realized how much she is part of this family now.” He turned to stare at the room. “You two want to make a road trip in the morning?” He sighed as his phone chimed. “Now what? It’s John. How did he know?”

“Know what?” Breck had approached.

“We’re heading to Littleton in the morning. John wants to go. We just made that decision.” Brendon’s eyes lifted, concern on them. He looked down at his phone and then handed it to Breck. “Have someone check this out, please? Someone is spying on us and it may be through that. I have felt that way for weeks.”

“And I’ll have the room here swept again. Security does it every day but we’ll pick up the number of times. This is just too coincidental.” Breck’s eyes never left Brendon’s face. “How far do you trust John?”

Brendon shrugged. “Not very, I would say. I mean, he seems to have been the one who brought me home, but how did he know where I was? And if he knew, why did it take so long? Do we have any proof that he’s who he says he is?”

“We have proof that he isn’t. The man that’s been around? That’s not John Dickerson.” Burnie held up a sheaf of papers from where he was seated near them. “Imly’s uncle is, I am sorry to say, deceased. He was run down a year or so ago, in that very village you are heading for, Brandon. His identification has been used over the last year, but what we can determine is that the man using it looks like him but it is an imposter."

"What about that material he gave us?" This from Benen.

"Emma took a look at it as has Dallas. It is all nonsense, they tell me." Branigan had risen, heading for the coffee pot, needing another cup of coffee.

"So, where do we stand, then?" Brendon rubbed at his forehead, a headache starting.

"Not where we were. We are making progress, Brendon, in spite of all the setbacks. Andy is flying Buckley and I back up to her hometown on Monday. There are some names we need to track down and people we need to talk to." Blair spoke from the end of the table, his head still bent over his papers. His voice died away before he was on his feet, the sheaf of papers in his hand. "Fellows, I think I know who is behind Wills." He looked up, seeing the expectant looks on his friends' faces before he looked at Barnabas. "Barnabas, how well does your father know Philip Baker?"

"Not that well. He's never felt comfortable around him, I know that. Mom avoids him. Is he the one?" Barnabas reached for the paper he was handed. "Is it him?"

"He's part of it. My research shows that he and Wills go back to school together, a boarding school, from the looks of it." Blair pointed to the paper. "There are notes there from what I could find. I have photos of them together that I saved to a file. I will pass it on to Dallas at some point, but for now, I'm holding on to it. Until or unless they escalate their attacks on you."

"That will happen." Brendon felt exhausted, his body sagging until his arms were braced for friends on either side of him. "Sorry, guys. I don't know what's wrong with me."

"You need to relax and get some sleep, Brendon. You Haven't this week." Breck reached for his arm, tugging him from the room. "If you're planning a trip tomorrow, how be we take you home and let you get some sleep? Imly may be awake by now and looking for you."

Chapter 34

Imly watched Devaney closely the next morning, a frown on her face, not quite sure why she was in her apartment. She sighed. I guess I have a babysitter, don't I, Lord? And then she sighed again. Forgive me, Lord. That's the wrong attitude. I know. I need to be thankful for friends who care. It's hard to praise in all this, but I'm trying.

Devaney watched Imly closely before she handed her the cup of tea she had ready for her.

"Here, Imly. Have a seat at your own table. And here's your peppermint tea I understand that you like. Forgive us if we have stepped in where we shouldn't have. I'll leave, and let you be."

Imly shook her head. "No, it's okay. I'm just not good company right now. Brendon explained it to me last night, what you ladies have planned, but I think I was too much out of it to really understand."

"It's okay. We tend to step in and out of one another's lives. We have all told each other off at times, asked for forgiveness, and moved on. I can't say that we have held grudges, not with what we have been through. Then, too, our fellows are close friends, and it would make it difficult if we were enemies."

Imly watched her closely. "I get that. I've never had a friend like that, you know? I mean, I have had friends, but none as close as you ladies are already."

"Oh, Imly. We didn't know that. I'm sorry."

"What's to be sorry for? You didn't know. I've been so used to it, that I didn't realize it could be different." Imly shifted uncomfortably. "Do you mind if we head for the living room? I think I'll be more comfortable there."

"Sure. What would you like to eat? Just some toast?"

"That would be great. And thank you."

Imly was asleep later that afternoon when Brendon returned, tired and spent, but with a sense of having accomplished something that day and he really needed to talk to his bride. He gave Devaney a quick hug as she was leaving with a thank you for staying and then headed to shower and change. He felt grubby, he thought.

Heading back for the kitchen, he could hear quiet sounds and stopped in the doorway, to watch Imly as she moved around, slowly to be sure, but on her feet. He approached her, talking to her as he did so.

Imly turned slowly, her hand resting on the counter, as she looked up at him, a smile breaking through the pain on her face.

"Did you have a good day, love?" He gently hugged her, holding on just a little bit longer, before he reached down to kiss her.

"I have no idea. Poor Devaney. I think I slept a lot of the day."

"She understands. She's been there, hurt and needing care." He pointed with his chin. "It seems that she has left a meal for us in the crockpot. How be I dish it up and set us up in the living room? You'll be more comfortable there."

"That would be great." Imly watched as he moved around his kitchen, content just to be near him. "How was your day?"

"Good. We managed to get the people in the village to talk to us. I need to go over what we found, but we need to eat first. Head on in, love. I'm right behind you."

Brendon finally wiped his mouth on the napkin he had been holding, before he rose to clean away their dishes, returning with her tea and his coffee. He sat beside her, an arm around her, as he bowed his head and prayed for the love of his life, knowing that when he spoke to her, it would change how she saw herself and her parents.

"Who's here tomorrow?" Brendon was delaying the talk, trying to frame his mind to put out the words in the way he needed to.

"I'm not sure. Hagen left a schedule on the fridge, I'm told." Imly's head went down on his shoulder, even as she yawned. "I hate pain medications. It makes me so sleepy. But, you found out something."

"I did. I didn't get a chance to talk to you last night. John, the man who claimed to be your uncle, is not him. We have confirmation that your uncle died a year or so again in an accident."

"He did? I wonder if Dad knew that. He hadn't seen or heard from him in years."

"I'm not sure. We can clarify that when we find your father." His voice dropped off, as he thought through the day. "What we found out is still to be verified, but we have confirmation of some of it. The fellows want to meet tomorrow, Sunday and all, just to work on it. It's okay, Imly. We've done it before. We'll do it again if we have to."

"And we will. Do you really think this stops with us?" Imly grew silent. "Somehow, sweetheart, hearing the stories of the adventures the other seven went through? It won't stop with us. It won't stop until it reaches Barnabas. Devaney mentioned that everyone felt something was missing in each of their investigations. I think that you'll find it ends up with Barnabas, that someone is after him, and is going after each one of you. It's as if someone targets us, someone hears about it and then starts working on that."

"I suspect you're right." Brendon was content for the moment just to sit quietly with Imly secure in his arms. "But we have to talk, Imly. I'm just not sure how to tell you what we found out."

———

Chapter 35

Finally speaking, Brendon tried to organize his thoughts in a way that made sense. Only, he thought, nothing makes sense about this.

"What did you find, sweetheart? It can't be any worse than what we already know." Imly's quiet confidence in him helped him to find the words.

"We went there, not really expecting to find out much. It was a long shot, as they say. The people had not been forthcoming when the other fellows stopped there. But it changed. When Bradon introduced me to the waitress in the family-style restaurant as your husband, that changed. She began to talk to us and drew others over to be introduced.

"It seems your father has an interest in that town. He spent time there as a child. That's why your uncle was there. He had gone home. I'll come back to him." Brendon paused, a prayer raising in his heart for what he had to say. "Anyway, we finally met the oldest person in town. A tiny little lady. She's a relative of yours, I think. She definitely wants to meet you. She gave us information on your family that I don't think you even know. She may be in her eighties but her mind is still razor-sharp."

"So, what did she have to say?" Imly waited, her head turned up to watch Brendon. "Brendon?"

Brendon shook his head to come back to the present. He had been lost in thought for a moment, wondering just where Imly's parents had gotten to.

"Your parents are not in that village, nor in the ones nearby. That much we determined. Your dad has been back there over the years, but he didn't have any contact with John. Apparently, John did not want to see him. I couldn't find out why. I was told I had to talk to your father about that. The impression left with us was that they had had a falling out of some sort and your uncle just refused to see your father."

"I can see that. Dad could be dogmatic about things. About the time Uncle John left, Dad had been in a bitter mood, unlike him. Mom wouldn't say what about. At the time, I was graduating high school, planning on college, and then a career."

"That's what Abigail told us. Your uncle had been specific with words about you. I am not sure if she would have opened up to you if you had been there."

Imly shrugged. "I don't know. I don't think it really matters now. What else?" She glanced towards the hallway as a tap came to the door. "Were we expecting anyone tonight?"

"Not that I know of." Brendon sighed, reached to kiss her, and then rose, heading for the door. He stared at Bradon and Brody and then past them at Breck. "Guys? Didn't you just go home?"

"We did, Brendon. But we have come across something that we need to talk to you two about." Bradon motioned towards the hall. "Can we come in?"

"Oh! Yeah, sure. We're in the living room. Coffee is on." Brendon turned and walked away, heading back for Imly, finding her almost asleep. "Imly? Some of the fellows are here. They need to talk to us."

"What? Can we do that tomorrow?"

"No, I think we should tonight. Can you stay awake for a while?" Brendon's arms were around her again, a quiet thank you to Breck for the refreshed mugs of coffee and tea that he placed on the table beside him.

"What do they need to know?" Imly squinted at them. "What do I have to tell you now?"

Bradon grinned. "This time, it's our turn to tell you something. We're hoping it's good news, but we're not even sure about that."

Imly shrugged, her head back on Brendon's shoulder, a sigh rising up from deep within her.

"If we must, we must." She yawned. "Sorry. The pain medication is working." She frowned. "Brendon, what did they give me this time? I thought it was a mild one. I can't handle heavy-duty ones."

Breck was on his feet heading for the kitchen, returning with the bottle in his hand. "It was a mild one." He popped the top from the bottle and shook one into his hand. "Imly, this is not what you were prescribed. I recognize this. This is too strong." He headed away, his phone out to call Dallas, leaving a voice mail for him, before he returned, setting the bottle beside him on the small table. "I'm taking these to give to Dallas. Brendon likely has something you can take."

"Thanks, Breck. Now, what did you find?" Brendon searched the faces of his friends, seeing a look on them that gave him hope they have found a clue that would lead to the end of this for them.

"We need to go back, Imly, Brendon. Back to when your father was young, Imly, around his mid-

———

172

teens from what we can determine." Bradon looked down at his notes. "Your father was raised in that village that we visited today. We have confirmed that. But Wills was also from around that area. They knew each other from high school. Wills was always a bully, even to this day."

Brody spoke up, picking up from Bradon's words. "Abigail called me a while ago, Brendon. She tried to call you, but couldn't get through. She wants to send us some more information, but I told her I'd go and get it. It's critical that we have what she has." He paused to sip at his coffee, trying to gather his thoughts. "She said that she had been mailed documents in the last few months from someone, no name on the envelopes, but it contained tax documents, shipping credentials, and other forms that she thought we should have. They have your father's name on them, but she seemed to think his signature was forged."

"Did she say where they were going to or coming from?" Imly sighed. "Those aren't the right words. Forgive me. I'm sorry. My brain is not functioning well tonight."

Brody grinned. "Understandable. We know what it's like, unfortunately. Now, about your father? Any other family members that we should know about?"

"I'm sure that you have discovered all of them. He had some cousins, but I have no idea where they are. If he has seen them in the last few years, I would not know that. As for Mom? She was the only child of an only child. That doesn't help, now does it?"

Chapter 36

Brendon finally locked the door after his three friends, his hand resting flat against it as he drew in a deep breath. They were still so far away, he thought, from finding out what was going on. He hadn't told Imly about the letter he had found taped to his vehicle that morning, a threat against her. Wills was still around, he was sure, or else he was paying someone.

"Brendon?" Imly's voice came from behind him and he spun around to face her, watching her closely.

"Yes, love?"

"Who did this? Who gave me the wrong medication? You had it filled at the pharmacy. Are they involved?" Imly walked into his arms, holding tightly to him.

"That's what we think. Breck is looking into that. He knows the owner of the pharmacy, but not all the pharmacists he has working for him. He spoke with Dallas just as they were leaving. Dallas is taking over that investigation as it is part of the bigger picture." He turned them to walk back towards the living room. "It doesn't end. We'll figure it out."

Imly sank back down on the couch, her arms wrapping around herself. "My mind is starting to clear a bit. It's been hours since I took one of those pills." She looked up as he sat beside her. "I guess church is out tomorrow."

"I think so. You're not able to sit for any length of time, that's a given." He reached for his Bible. "We can do our own church. But for now, let's just spend some time reading our favourite verses and praying."

"I would like that. I miss that." She leaned against him. "Thank you, Brendon, for being who you are. That is one thing I can praise God for in all of this."

Waking early the next morning, Brendon rose and moved around the apartment quietly, finally dropping down into his desk chair, reaching for the computer mouse to wake up his computer. He read through his emails, responding to Lawrence's questions, and then pulled up the file he had been working on.

He added the notes that he made from the day before and then sat back, studying what he had written. Brendon was frustrated. There had to be a better way to sort this. He looked up as he felt a hand on his shoulder and then wrapped an arm around Imly to pull her down onto his lap, kissing her before she could react.

"Brendon? You're up early." She looked at his computer monitor. "What are you making?"

"A mess, I think. I don't know what to do with this."

"Let me look at it. Can you print it? It's sometimes easier to look at something in black and white. And then we can scribble all over the pages."

"Scribble, is it? Do you have crayons?" He grinned as she gave him a playful swat.

"No, I don't but different colours would be a good idea. How many colours of pens and highlighters do you have?"

"Not enough. I know there are plenty in the conference room." He reached for a thumb drive, to transfer the file to it. "We can move down there after breakfast." He sat back, his eyes on her face. "You look much brighter and in less pain this morning."

"I think I am. My mind is not foggy like it was. What was I given?"

"Dallas hasn't responded to that question just yet. Whatever it is, when we find out, you'll never be given it again."

Hours later, Imly stood and stretched, a hand resting over her incision. Doc had been by, to ensure that she was not overdoing it, and she knew Brady was keeping a close eye on her. Brody had returned with the documentation from Abigail and had made copies of it all for each one, putting the originals back into the envelope to hand over to Dallas.

Ennis and Fynn approached Imly, drawing her away and to Fynn's apartment. Brendon watched her leave before he turned back to Burnie, frowning at the paper that the other man kept shoving at him.

"What is this, Burnie?"

"This? This is a crucial part of the evidence, I think, Brendon. I checked the signatures with what Imly provided. This is her father's. It is on a customs form shipping jewels to Ireland. Did he know what he was doing?"

"What's the date?" Brendon drew in a deep breath. "This is three days after Imly disappeared. Did they do this to try and get her back?"

"That is something that we'll need to ask them, if we ever find them." Burnie sat back, his eyes thoughtful. "I just don't get it, Brendon. Where are they? Are they involved after all and in hiding? Or are they being held hostage or captive or what?"

"That I don't know." Brendon looked up as Branigan sat down beside him. "Branigan? I don't like the look on your face."

"I don't like to be the bearer of bad news. Remember how we had DNA testing done? Barnabas was able to get a rush on it." Branigan looked down at the papers he held. "We got the results back. Imly and her parents? Their DNA does not match. I'm sorry, Brendon. It's not what we had hoped."

"No, but it is what we expected." Brendon reached for the paperwork. "I'll talk to her tonight. Right now, she's with the ladies. She needs that. Devaney was almost in tears today when she spoke with me. She said Imly had admitted that she never really had a close friend, not like the ladies are here."

"That makes sense, in a sick way." Brennen had sat down at the table. "They would want to keep her away from too many people, just in case someone found out that she wasn't theirs. How do we find out who she really is?"

"We discussed this, Imly and I. She is adamant that Imly is her correct name. Her birthdate seems to be correct, from what she can figure out." Brendon sat back, before he was on his feet, heading for a box that had been packed up from Imly's home and brought back. "Imly had the fellows pack everything up, paperwork and all. I don't think we've gone through it." He was pulling off the tape and opening the box flaps as he spoke.

"Here. Let us all take some. There's a lot there. Hopefully, we can sort this out."

Chapter 37

Late that evening, Brendon ventured back into his office, a frown on his face as he thought of the conversation that he and Imly had had over their dinner. Imly was not surprised at the DNA results, disappointed, she admitted, but questioning who and why. And how was Wills involved in it all, she had asked, and who was behind him and that.

Brendon reached to flick on the desk lamp, pausing for a moment at the gift-wrapped package on his desk. Shooting a glance towards the door, he carefully unwrapped it, opening the flaps on the box, a delighted grin on his face as he stared down into it before he began to laugh. He carefully lifted out the large box of crayons, then the large box of colouring pencils, the huge number of coloured pens and markers. Imly had been busy, he thought. Who would have done this? Then, his grin widened. Darbie, he thought, Darbie, Haley, and Hollie. He had thought they had been up to something. Now he knew what.

He sank into his chair, bracing his elbows on the desktop, his chin resting on his clasped hands. Where do we go from here, Lord? I feel like we have hit a dead end. Do we turn around and head back the way we came or do we find a tangent to follow?

Looking up at the clock, Brendon was shocked to see it was after three in the morning. He stared down at the papers he had been working out, colour coding them as Imly had requested. It was beginning to make sense, he thought. He had traced back the couple who had raised her, finding discrepancies in their information that he needed to talk to the fellows and Dallas or even Will about. He also had a fair idea of where she was from. And that concerned him. A small village should have been aware that a child disappeared and sounded the alarm, but it would appear that none had gone out. Who had prevented that?

Rising from his chair, he padded through to the kitchen, where he had left on a low light and reached for the coffee pot, to rinse it out and make fresh. He didn't think he would be sleeping that night. He yawned widely, rubbing at the back of his neck, before he wandered through the apartment, trying to see it from Imly's point of view and just not doing that. Brendon wanted her to make changes, had asked her to, but she had just looked at him. For now, she was content, she said, to live in it as he had decorated it. It would come, she promised, once she was feeling better and could see what they needed.

He stood for a moment, watching her sleep before he stooped to drop a kiss on her cheek. He was so thankful she was in his life. Turning away, he headed for the kitchen and his mug of coffee and then back to the office.

Finally, throwing down his pen and rubbing at his tired, bloodshot eyes, Brendon felt confident that he knew who was behind it all. And that person lived here in his town. And had been in his hometown. So, he thought, who was this person really after? Was it him or Imly? It really didn't make sense, he thought, that this person had tracked him down. He hadn't known Imly until the day she appeared in the shop. Of that, he was certain.

Imly stood for a moment in the shadows of the dimly-lit hallway, watching Brendon as he worked away. He's discovered something, hasn't he, Lord? Is this where we praise You, for letting him find something? I guess it is. She moved quietly away, heading for the living room, searching for her phone. Scrolling through the messages, she stopped at one. Her father, or who she thought had been her father, had sent a text message. One that really didn't make a lot of sense.

Jumping as she felt someone near her, she spun, directly into Brendon's arms, her phone trapped between them.

"Good morning, love. Sleep well?"

"I think so. You didn't, did you?"

"No, I worked all night." He looked down at her. "Let me shower and change, and then I'll let you know what I have been up to." He grinned suddenly as he swooped down to kiss her. "Thank you for the gift."

"Gift? What gift?" Imly was puzzled.

"The one on my desk. You know, the one with the crayons, pencil crayons, pens, markers?" He frowned at her puzzled look. "You didn't know?"

Imly began to smile. "No, I didn't. But Hollie was around when I was telling the ladies about how I had threatened to get you them. She must have."

"Hollie, and Haley, and Darbie. They can get up to mischief when they're together, but never anything bad." He kissed her again before walking away, leaving her staring after him, her face rosy with a blush.

Hearing a tap at the door, she frowned, thinking that she was frowning a lot. Standing on tiptoes, she peeked through the peephole, seeing Breck standing there, his attention on someone beside him.

"Breck?" Imly peeked around the door she had opened. "It's early. Didn't you sleep either?"

Breck grinned. "And who didn't sleep here?"

"I did. It was Brendon. He's been colouring in his office all night." She grinned, knowing that Brendon was standing right behind her.

"He has been, has he?" Breck held up the papers he had in his hand. "Then, maybe he needs these. And this is Gus Wilson. He's an investigator who Barnabas contacted. He has some interesting information for you."

"Come in then, Breck." Brendon reached to draw Imly back from the door. "What do you have?" He led the way to his office, an arm around Imly to draw her with him.

"As I said, interesting material."

Chapter 38

Pacing the conference room, Brendon watched his friends closely as they intently worked away, quiet conversation sparse at best. He was frustrated, he had to admit, but at least they were making progress. He stopped beside Brody, who had risen and headed for the map on the wall, placing another blue dot on it.

"A blue dot, Brody? What are all the dots for?" Brendon's index finger touched them.

Brody grinned. "Darbie suggested that, muttering something about you colour coding things. The blue dots are where Ian Dickerson has been over the years. Does Imly know he is that well-traveled?"

"Imly didn't know that. He would be way for a day, a couple of days, sometimes a week, but he always said it was to do with his woodworking." Imly spoke up from behind the men. "Why?" Her eyes widened as she saw the number of blue dots. "Those are all from his trips?"

"Just the ones that Emma has been able to verify. She says there are many more they are working on. Did you know he traveled like that?"

"No, I didn't. I guess I never thought much about it." Imly chewed at her finger. "When I was little, I never really paid that much attention, I don't think. As a teenager, I really didn't care. When I started working, I had no interest in his travels. I was concerned about making good and then finding my own place." She paced behind the men. "What else is there to learn?"

"We're working on it, Imly." Brody looked down for a moment. "I have to say this. I am sorry this happened to you. It shouldn't have."

"Thank you, Brody. But I know that God allowed it. For whatever reason, He placed me there." She looked up at the ceiling, blinking rapidly. "Do we know anything more about my past?" At their silence, she looked back at them and then turned to look at the other men, surprised to find them all standing around her and Brendon, the ladies there as well. "What?"

"Brendon found some information that he wanted us to verify. He was not going behind your back, Imly." Brennen spoke for the group. "He wanted to be sure of his facts before he approached you. Brendon?"

Brendon nodded, his hands reaching to pull Imly close to him, to wrap her in a hug. "Buckley?"

Buckley nodded, knowing exactly what Brendon was asking. As the heads were bowed, he prayed, for Imly, for Brendon, for her real parents, for themselves and also Dallas. He prayed for resolution of the mystery surrounding her, and that God would be praised in all things.

Imly's head raised, a determined look on her face. "Brendon?"

"I have managed to trace you back to where you came from. It's a small village not far from here. Not the one that John and the man calling himself your father came from. That was a red herring, we think." He paused, wrapping his arms tighter around her. "I asked Emma to do some research. And her friend,

Kataleen, helped with her family tree program. We have found the lost child posters, the reports of you being missing and likely abducted. Why you were never found, we don't know. They were sent out province-wide."

"I don't understand, Brendon. Who am I?" Imly turned slowly in a circle, her eyes searching each face around her. "Brendon?"

"You really are Imly Anna Dickerson. Your birthdate is the one you have always celebrated. Why they did this, we may never know. Dallas is working hard on the trail of them in his investigation. He called when you were out with the ladies a bit ago. He has information that he wants to verify. Then, he will be by." Brendon hugged her tight to him. "I'm so sorry, Imly. I wish it had been different for you. So much was stolen from you."

Imly drew a deep breath. "Thank you, sweetheart. Now what?" The friends around them could hear the devastation in her voice and see it on her face, noting that she was blinking rapidly to contain the tears she refused to shed.

"Now, we finalize everything we can, turn it over to Dallas, and protect you at the same time. He said that he had been warned someone other than Wills was looking for you." Breck spoke up. He turned to the others. "Let's go, fellows. Let's solve this today, if we can. Imly deserves to be free of what has been hanging over her for years.'"

The men scattered, the ladies as well, to find seats, the rustle of papers sounding loud in the room. Imly watched from where she still stood in the shelter of Brendon's arms before she turned back to the map.

———

185

"What were you planning on finding, Brendon?"

He shrugged. "I wasn't sure, love. I was just finding all these places. Why?"

"Has anybody researched thefts, or drug busts, insurance claims in these places?" Imly moved away from him, a finger tracing the dots. "It's like we're trying to connect the dots, as they say, whoever they are. Will it lead to the one behind it all? Someone other than Wills? Someone in the insurance game?" She spun, determination on her face, a sparkle back in her eyes. "I remembered something. I wasn't supposed to be home but I heard them talking. Something about insurance fraud and theft. I had forgotten, I guess thinking it didn't really matter. But it does, doesn't it?"

"It does, love. Come. Sit with me. We'll start looking at that angle. I'm sure one of the fellows is working on it as well."

Barnabas had been nearby as they spoke, his hand reaching for the coffee pot, before he paused, setting his mug down. He turned so he could watch Imly, the overhead light catching her profile. He drew in a deep breath. He knew who she reminded him of. But, how did he prove it?

Chapter 39

The conference room door closing quietly behind him, Barnabas walked rapidly towards his office, nodding at Amy as he entered.

"What paperwork do I need to look after for you?"

"You're all caught up for now. You must have been in here early this morning." Amy smiled and shook her head at him.

"I was. For some reason, I felt compelled to be here. I also spent a good portion of time in prayer." He looked down for a moment, his fingers rubbing together. "You've talked to Dad and Mom. Do you know if they're planning on stopping by soon? I've only gotten voice mail when I try."

"I have. They have no plans, not before the board meeting in a couple of weeks. And then it would just be your Dad. You're missing them."

"I am, Amy. This bit with Imly? It has really driven in how fortunate I am to have my parents. The fellows don't and that saddens me."

"I know it does. Go. Phone your parents. I'm done for now. Do you need anything?"

"No, thanks, Amy. Take off and enjoy your evening."

Barnabas sank into his chair, his phone turning over and over in his hands, before he dialled the familiar number.

———

"Hi, Dad."

"Barnabas!" Bruce Carey's voice echoed over the phone to his son. "You've been calling and Haven't been able to reach us. We were away to the island." Bruce referred to the island in the lake near where they lived, which had a cottage they occasionally ventured to.

"Were you, Dad? I wish I could join you."

"You should, son. You need some time away." Bruce asked about the men and the ladies before his voice died away. "You called about something in particular, didn't you, son?"

"I did, Dad. Ian and Emily Dickerson. Do you still see them?"

"We do. In fact, they are here now. Why?"

"What do you remember about their daughter? I seem to recall them mentioning they had a daughter, but she is not around." Barnabas almost held his breath.

"Their daughter? That's interesting that you would ask. They were speaking of her today, missing her greatly. They never really knew what happened. For all their searching, they never found her."

"Dad, I am going to send you a photo. Will you take a look at it for me?" Barnabas sent the text with the photo off to his father and then waited, a prayer in his heart that he was right.

"Barnabas? Where did you get the picture of Emily?" Bruce was puzzled.

"It's not Emily, Dad. It's a lady, Brendon's wife, in fact, who has become involved in one of those adventures. We Haven't had a chance to speak, other than sending our emails. Does she look like Emily?"

"She does. It is incredible. This is what Emily looked like when she was around thirty. Who is she?"

Barnabas could hear his mother's voice speaking with his father. "Dad, are you two by yourselves? If so, put your phone on speaker, please. Mom?"

"Barnabas? I don't understand. Your Dad says this is Brendon's wife. She looks like Emily."

"I think she is their missing daughter. What was her name?"

"Imly." Bruce spelt it for him. "It's unusual, but they wanted something close to her mother's without it being identical."

"Then, she is here. Brendon's Imly, we have discovered, was kidnapped as a young child. I don't know all the details that the men and in particular, Brendon, have discovered, but they have proof that Imly was that child. Brendon has even been able to track back to the village she was from. He can't explain how it happened. He said a name or an idea would cross his mind and he would follow that tangent. It has to be God, Dad, Mom." Barnabas grew silent.

"And we need to tell them, and then get them there. Son, I will leave it to you to discuss with Brendon and then tell Imly. We'll work on our part up here. Knowing Ian and Emily, they'll want to head there tomorrow."

"They will, I guess. Dad, one other thing? The couple who raised Imly? They were murdered. Imly was kidnapped and brought down to our town, finally escaping and then hiding in Lawrence's shop, where

Brendon discovered her. We'll let you know the rest when you get in."

"We'll be praying, son. Have no doubt about that." Bruce clicked off his phone, a thoughtful look on his face, before he looked up at Elizabeth. "Lizzie, we need to talk to them."

"We do, but first we pray."

They moved at last towards their back yard, finding Ian and Emily walking towards them. Bruce hesitated before he spoke.

"Ian? Emily? How be we have a seat in the house? Barnabas has called."

"Barnabas? How is he? And the men? How many are married now?" Ian's smile lit his face as he thought of Barnabas. "It's been a long while since we saw him."

"It has been, Ian. Here, Lizzie, let me take the tray for you." Bruce headed for the sunroom, a room they used a lot.

Ian finally set his mug down, his eyes on his long-time friend. "Bruce? Something is troubling you."

Bruce drew a deep breath, a prayer raising in his heart. "There is. Barnabas called for a reason." He reached into his pocket for his phone, drawing up the photo that Barnabas had sent him. "He called asking about you two. He also sent a photo on to me, one that I would like you to take a look at." He looked up at Lizzie. "First, let's pray. If it is what I think it is, it will rock your world."

Chapter 40

Finally handing his phone to Ian, Bruce sat back, his hands lightly clasped, his eyes on his friends. Elizabeth linked her arm with his as she too watched them.

Ian shot Bruce a look, one of puzzlement, before he looked at his wife. She shrugged and then tilted his hand to look at the photo, a shocked sound coming from her.

"Bruce? This is me, I think. How did he get this photo?" Emily studied it closer. "No, it's not me. It's too modern. Who is she?"

Ian's mouth worked as he tried to control his emotions, tears momentarily blinding him before he spoke, his voice barely audible.

"Imly!"

"What?" Emily stared at him.

"It's Imly, darling. All grown up. She always did look like you." He drew a deep breath, his arm around her. "Bruce? What is the meaning of this?"

"It's a long story, Ian. But apparently, she showed up, Brendon rescued her, fell in love and married her. Barnabas didn't go into all the details, but for now, she is safe. Brendon has traced her back to your village."

"I don't understand. Where has she been?" Emily stared at the phone, her finger coming out to trace Imly's face. "I want to see her."

"We'll take you there. I told Barnabas that you would want to go tomorrow?"

"Tomorrow? Tonight!" Ian's voice was forceful.

"Tomorrow. We need to let Brendon have time to talk to Imly and warn her that you are coming. She has just found out that she is a missing child, the couple who raised her are dead. By the way, the man used your name, Ian."

That same evening, Brendon had gone looking for Imly, finding her curled up on the love seat in his office, a forlorn look on her face. She didn't move when he sat beside her, reaching to pull her over to him and just hold her.

"Brendon? Why?" He could hear the suppressed tears in her voice. This has rocked her world, as they say, he thought.

"I don't know, love. That's what we're working on. Dallas called earlier when you were cleaning up the kitchen. He's not going to make it today after all. He's tied up on another case for the night. He sends his apologies."

Imly shrugged. "I didn't expect that he would come." Her head dropped onto his shoulder. "Where do we go from here? How do we find my parents? Are they even alive? And would they even want anything to do with me after all these years? I am sure they have moved on."

"That's something we need to talk about. First, though, we need to pray. I miss my parents are times like this. It's hard being an orphan." He prayed for them, knowing that when he talked to her, it would change what she thought of things and people.

Imly finally spoke. "You wanted to talk to me, Brendon?"

"I do." He paused, not quite sure how to proceed. "The fellows took what I had done, followed more of a trail, confirming names and dates. I wanted to be sure before we talked." He paused, biting at his lip, trying to sort out his thoughts. "I found your parents, Imly."

She was quiet, not sure that she had heard him right. Her face raised to his. "Did you say that you found them?"

"I did. They still live in that village. From what we can determine, they have never lost hope of finding you. The detectives have been working on your case on and off over the years, not willing to let it go to a cold, unsolved case." He paused again, a slight smile on his face that Imly frowned at. "But there is more. Barnabas took a photo of you this morning and sent it on to his father, whom you have not met yet. Bruce confirmed that friends of theirs are your parents. In fact, Barnabas said they were staying with them today."

"They are? He did? How?"

"His Dad and Mom took one look at you and asked where he got the photo of Emily. That's your Mom's name. They showed the photo to their friends, and they were shocked. Your father confirmed it was you. If we need to, we have the DNA testing that we did. And I guess they had submitted DNA testing to some missing children's site."

"Oh, Brendon? Really? You found them. Thank you." She reached to kiss him before snuggling back down. "I guess we need to meet then. When do we leave?"

<hr>

"We don't." His finger came across her lips as she went to protest. "Bruce said your father wanted to head down here today. He convinced them to wait until tomorrow, to let us talk to you and prepare you."

"Thank you." Imly grew silent, sorrow in her heart over the years that had been missed with her real parents. She finally spoke, talking at length about her childhood, how sheltered she had been kept, how she had few friends, that the couple who had raised her had frowned on her leaving home at all. Her words spent at long last, she turned her face against him and slept, shedding tears that soaked his shirt, breaking his heart for his beloved Imly.

Chapter 41

Early the next morning, Barnabas stood in his open apartment door, watching his parents and the Dickersons walking towards him. Doc stood just outside his door. Barnabas had asked him to be handy, if he could, and he readily agreed.

Hugged by his parents, Barnabas reached to shake Ian's hand, only to find himself swept into a tight hug by the other man and then hugged even tighter by Emily, a whispered, tear-filled thank you in his ear.

"Dad? You made good time."

"We did. Andy flew up early this morning. He called for something else and then when I said we were heading down, he volunteered to come. He's been that concerned about Imly."

"He has been. He was one of the ones who went north." Barnabas beckoned them in. "I have breakfast just about ready. We'll eat, spend some time in prayer and then go find Imly and Brendon."

"Brendon?" His mother shook her head, a smile on her face. "I never thought he would marry. He's been so much of a big brother to the girls here."

"He has been, Mom, but he has found the one lady who completes him." Barnabas waited until they had finished eaten and the table and kitchen cleaned up before he spoke again. He detailed how Imly and Brendon had met, what had transpired just prior to that, and what the couple had faced.

Ian and Emily's faces grew grave and tense, hearing what had happened to their daughter.

"She's okay now, Barnabas?" Ian's voice was barely audible, his emotions that much in play.

"She's getting there. She tells me that she still tires easily and the headaches can come and go, but overall, Doc here says she's better."

"Ian, Emily, I can't tell you from a medical standpoint what happened with Imly. I have treated her and can't break that confidence. But I can say she has healed remarkably well. Even when Brendon was missing, she had to be told to rest, to heal, and fought us on that at times."

The five finally rose, heading for the conference room, standing just outside the door Barnabas opened. They watched the activity in there, heard the quiet comments, and then gentle teasing and laughter. Ian and Emily exchanged glances, not having been aware this was what the men had done.

"This is normal now for the fellows. Dad and Mom, we'll go in first, I think. We need to let Brendon know Ian and Emily are here."

Brendon looked up as a hand touched his shoulder and he rose, a hand out to shake Bruce's before Elizabeth hugged him.

"Brendon? I hear you have been having one of those adventures that you fellows seem to think you need to have."

Brendon grinned. "I have been. We told the others that it stopped with Brandon, but it didn't. Good to see you two again. Imly's upstairs with the ladies. She's extremely nervous." He rubbed his hands together. "And so am I. There is a lot riding on this."

———

196

"There is, but God has gone before us. Listen, Ian and Emily are waiting outside the room with Doc. Come, meet them." Bruce turned Brendon, towards the door, nodding to the other men who had risen and then followed them.

Ian stood, an arm around Emily, watching the door closely, a sigh drawn from him when only Brendon approached him, Bruce and Barnabas on either side of the younger man.

"Brendon, is it?" Ian spoke first.

"It is, sir. I am so sorry for what you two went through. You have missed a lot. Your daughter is a wonderful, compassionate, caring lady who I love deeply." Brendon didn't know that his words had helped to ease the worry and burden the Dickersons had carried for close to twenty-five years.

"Thank you." Emily reached to hug him. "God bless you, son."

Brendon looked past her, gave a small sound and excused himself, long strides taking him to Imly. She stood, her eyes on Ian and Emily as they watched the younger couple before she looked up at Brendon, a woebegone look on her face, a lostness to her that broke his heart. He swept her to him and then turned her away, taking her outside to a bench in a nearby garden, nodding to the security guards who had followed.

"Talk to me, Imly." He waited for her to speak, letting her have the time she needed.

"Was that them, Brendon?"

He nodded. "It was. They really want to meet you, but I only allow it if you are agreeable. If you can't today, we don't. It is entirely up to you." He raised his eyes to see Imly's parents waiting nearby, Barnabas and his parents beside them, and behind them, his friends standing in solidarity with Brendon and Imly, the ladies standing in front of their men.

"I know we need to, Brendon, but I'm scared. I am so scared. What if whoever it is that is after me goes after them? How do I live with myself if they are hurt?"

"They have been hurt, and have been for years. You three need to heal. But I won't push you. Let God lead you in what you do. I will stand beside you and behind you, whatever your decision is. If you need me to speak for you, I will. If you want to walk away and move somewhere else, that's what we'll do."

Imly looked at him in horror. "You can't do that, Brendon. This is your home. Your work is here. So are your friends."

"You are the most important one right now. They understand that. The ones who are married? They have all felt the same." He looked up, staring into the distance. "I want to do what is best for you. You are the most important person in my life, next to God."

Imly leaned against him, a deep sigh that was almost a sob rising from her. "I guess that I can meet them. I'm just so nervous."

"And they are." He looked down at her, his heart breaking, wanting to prevent any more hurt for her, but knowing that he could not. "When you are ready, we'll go meet them."

"Are they out here?"

Brendon laughed. "They are, and so is everyone else. They are that concerned for you, but

———

198

also pulling for you to find your family and become whole again."

"Is that what this will do? Will it fill that spot deep inside me that I couldn't ever fill or get rid of?" She finally stood, her eyes on him. "Let's go, Brendon. At least, let me meet them. Whatever happens, God is in control. I can only praise Him that He is."

Brendon stood, hugging her, and then dropping a kiss on her forehead, a prayer whispered in her ear. "If you are sure, then I will walk beside you, every step of the way. You will not go forward into anything without me."

"Thank you, Brendon. I love you." Her whispered words warmed his heart, even as he echoed them back to her, before he turned her to face the ones who were waiting for her, desperate to reach out and touch her, to love her once more.

Chapter 42

Her eyes on the couple as she walked forward towards them, her hand tight in Brendon's, Imly drew a deep breath. She was shocked to see how much like the woman she looked.

"Brendon? I look like her."

"You do. It's uncanny how much you do." He stopped their forward walk, staying a few feet apart from the couple. "Imly, this is Ian and Emily. Ian and Emily, Imly."

Emily's hand covered her mouth as she sobbed, Ian's arms around her, tears on his face. The shock of finally seeing their daughter after so many years shook them both to their core, leaving them unable to speak.

Imly was puzzled for a moment before she spoke.

"Hi! I feel like I should know you, but I don't."

"That's understandable." Ian had to clear his throat before he continued. "It's been too many years, Imly. Too much has happened. But, this? You are here. Back in front of us. A lady grown, a beautiful one at that."

Imly nodded, her eyes on her mother as she listened. "Thank you. I'm sorry. I'm so sorry. I'm sorry they put you through all this." She looked up with a frown as a sudden buzzing sounded, a scream breaking from her as Brendon swept her away from the couple and to the ground, his body covering hers. They could hear the commotion and shouts of the others, even as an explosion sounded close to them, shaking their bodies violently.

Shouts rang through the area, even as the men scrambled back to their feet, the ladies running for the building, Ian and Emily with them, Elizabeth holding the door for everyone. She stood, heart in her mouth, as she watched Bruce and Barnabas outside. They could hear the sounds of the sirens as the emergency vehicles approached.

Doc was on his knees beside the young couple, Brady beside him, hands reaching to move Brendon away from Imly, to assess them. Barnabas squatted beside them.

"Doc?"

"They're okay, Barnabas. Just had the breath knocked out of them. Brendon?"

Brendon nodded, a hand on his chest, the other on his head. "Doc? What happened?"

"An explosive device of some kind." Breck crouched down near them. "You're okay?"

"I think so. Imly?" Brendon shook away the hands reaching to help him sit up, instead rolling to his side and reaching for Imly.

"Brendon? Where are we?" Imly's eyes were not focused, concerning him.

"We're at home, love. Someone just dropped a bomb near us."

"They did? Why? Who would do that?" She sat up carefully, frowning for a moment. "I'm having trouble seeing."

"Imly?" Doc's voice was stern as he spoke. "Can you look at me?"

"I would if you would stop moving and there weren't so many of you."

"Sounds like a concussion. We'll need to take you in." Brady stood, ready to help her to the stretcher wheeled nearby, when she shook her head, a grimace covering her face.

"Why did you make me do that?" She grumbled, even as the men around her grinned at her comment. "No, I need to go lie down, I think. Brendon, please?"

"That we will do. We'll take you to the infirmary here. Doc and Brady will watch out for you, but you will go in and be assessed if you don't come around soon." He stood, on shaky legs before he stopped and swept her into his arms, heading for the building, a wall of men around him.

Dallas stood watching. He had been on his way out there when word reached him that an attempt was planned on Imly's life that day at the building. He had requested backup and it was those sirens that Elizabeth had heard.

Emily and Ian followed closely behind him, concern and fear on their faces, watching as Brendon laid Imly down on the bed before he tried to step back, Imly's hand grabbing for his arm, preventing him from doing just that.

"Brendon? Don't leave me !" She blinked. "Who else is here?"

"Doc. Brady. Anna. And Ian and Emily."

"They're here? I thought they had left, that they didn't want me." Sobs shook her body, increasing her headache, even as Brendon swept her close to him, his cheek resting against her.

"No, love. They didn't leave. They are wanting to spend time with you." He finally set her back, stepping away, motioning for Ian and Emily to approach.

Emily stopped beside the bed, a hand out that she kept drawing back before she dared lay it against the red hair so close in colour to her own.

"Imly?"

Imly started, her face turning towards Emily. "Mom? Where have you been? I looked for you, but I couldn't find you. I was so scared. They wouldn't let me go." Imly began to sob, deep heart-wrenching sobs that shook her body, bringing tears to Emily's eyes as she gathered her daughter to her arms, glad to have her there, but missing all the years they had been apart. Ian's arms surrounded his ladies, his own face wet with tears.

Brendon stepped back and then from the room, to stand with an arm folded against the wall, his face burned against it, as sobs shook his own body. His friends shared looks of compassion for him, even as Bruce approached, an arm going around Brendon just as he would his own son. Bruce considered all the men his family and would treat them no less than that.

Brendon finally roused enough to hear Bruce's prayer for him, knowing that his lady was back with her family. But just where that left them, he wasn't sure.

Chapter 43

Looking around later that afternoon, Brendon frowned at the footsteps he could hear. They didn't sound familiar. He was on his feet, heading for the door to the infirmary room where Imly still slept, when he slid to a sudden halt, his hands rising in the air. He backed away until the hospital bed stopped him.

"What do you want? I think you have the wrong building." He frowned at the men standing in front of him.

"No, we don't. We're in the right place." The speaker, a heavyset man that reminded Brendon of Wills, spoke before he pointed towards Imly. "She's the one we want. She's going with us."

"I don't think so." Brendon's hands clenched, ready to protect his lady.

"Oh, I think so. Move." The man beckoned to one of the men with him when Brendon made no movement away from the bed.

A sudden blow across his face had Brendon stumbling sideways, a hand out to catch himself from tumbling to the floor, the other hand reaching to wipe the blood from his mouth.

"I'm not leaving her. And you're not leaving with her." Brendon straightened back up, his hands raised and clenched, ready to fight for his lady, despite being outnumbered.

A few minutes later, the man stepped away from Brendon, leaving him crumpled and unconscious on the floor, the beating brutal at times. The leader nodded and then approached the bed, staring at Imly dispassionately before he spoke.

"Take her." When his men didn't respond, he repeated himself. Uncertain as to why there was no movement around him, he began to turn and halted quickly, feeling the small round end of a gun barrel against his back.

"I don't think so. She's not going anywhere. You are." Dallas reached for his cuffs and snapped them around the man's wrists. "For starters, Tyron Wills, you are under arrest for conspiracy to commit assault, threatening, attempted kidnapping. There is a slew of other charges just waiting to be laid. You won't be taking anyone anywhere." He nodded to the officers, who filed out with their prisoners.

Doc was on his knees beside Brendon, finding him moving, pain on his face as he did so.

"Brendon, here let's get you on your feet. I need to look you over." Doc helped him to stand, an arm around him to steady him.

"Imly?" Brendon tried to move away from Doc, to approach Imly.

"She's still sleeping, Brendon. Here, down in this chair." Doc worked quickly, quiet words to Brady who helped. "God was looking over you today, Brendon. You're bruised and battered, but considering everything, fortunate you didn't have any wore damage done to you."

"Imly?" Brendon finally shoved away their hands, stood, and approached Imly, finding her just rousing. "Imly, love."

———

"Brendon?" She squinted at him. "What did you do? You look like you've been in a fight and lost."

"That's about what happened. You're safe, love. Dallas is here."

"Imly?" Dallas spoke from beside her. "We have them all now. Brendon is correct. You are safe. At last, you are safe."

"I am? I'm so sorry, Dallas, to have made all this work for you." Imly drifted off, leaving Brendon shaking his head, and grinning at Dallas.

"Did she really just apologize?"

"She did, Dallas. She does that. For some reason, she feels that she has to. She can't explain it."

Dallas just shook his head, commented that she was certainly unique, and walked away, stating he would be around the next day. He definitely had to talk to them.

Brendon looked up as he felt an arm around him. Emily stood there, hugging him, Ian on his other side, an arm around his shoulder.

"Welcome to the family, Brendon." Ian had trouble getting his words out. To have found his daughter and then almost had her disappear again had shaken him badly.

Chapter 44

Searching the faces gathered around them in the conference room the next day, Imly snuggled closer to Brendon, his arm around her, her hand in her mother's. The couple had spent the morning with her parents, getting to know one another, to talk over what had happened, to weep with one another but more importantly, to spend time in prayer and praise.

Dallas looked up from his papers, nodding to Barnabas, who looked at his father. Bruce rose to his feet, his voice raised in prayer and also praise as well, bringing them into God's presence with his words, asking for understanding and a blessing on all that had gathered.

Dallas finally began to speak. "Imly? I know this has been so difficult for you. To find out that you were kidnapped as a child, not aware of that, losing the couple that had raised you, to be kidnapped and then suffer as you have with physical assaults and having Brendon disappear as he did? I cannot fathom how you have kept your spirit in an attitude of praise. That was certainly God at work.

"Now, to go to Wills, the younger brother, the one who had you kidnapped and brought down here. He had threatened the couple who had raised you. Tyron Wills had you kidnapped at age three, placed you with them, telling them that you were an orphan. He saw you outside your home and took the opportunity to have his men take you. He apparently searched for a couple who bored the same name as one of your parents and found one who was named Ian.

They were a Christian couple, but Tyron Wills had information on a crime that the man had committed and gotten away with before his conversion. He used this as blackmail, forcing him to use his woodworking skills to prepare furniture and boxes and whatever else you remember to be used in smuggling jewels, artwork, documents, and even drugs out of the country. All of these were stolen. When you asked about insurance fraud and theft, this was part of it. We are working with the federal officials here and with officials overseas to try and recover what we can. It will be a long process.

"Brendon, when you rescued Imly and then married her, you became a target. Wills for some reason decided that Imly had an inheritance coming to her. He was led to believe this by his brother. He never worked in this town, not in a legitimate business at any rate. We have arrested all the men that were involved in everything you two went through."

"This John? Who was he?" Brendon was puzzled.

"John? That's a mystery, Brendon. We can't find anyone who knows him or has seen him. It is as if he is a ghost."

"Or an angel." Imly's head went against Brendon's arm. "It is possible, but God placed him where He needed him, to rescue Brendon and bring him home."

Dallas clarified what little he could, stating simply that it was still an ongoing investigation and that he would be around, just to keep them all updated on what he was finding. And yes, he stated, they would be required to appear in court, to testify at some point.

Mingling with his friends, Brendon felt fatigued, his body sore and bruised from the beating he had taken the day before. He stopped beside Breck, not saying anything.

"Brendon? Any regrets?" Breck's voice was quiet.

Brendon shrugged. "I guess I do. But I'm not sure how to exactly express them."

"That's fair." Breck nodded towards where Imly stood with Emily and Elizabeth. "This is what we do. And we praise God when we do. Listen, Barnabas is going to talk to you, but he asked if I would give you a head's up. He wants to send you to school, to learn investigations. He would like to set up a section of the Foundation to find missing children. The board is agreeable, quite eager in fact. Your name has been raised by all of them as the one to head it. Only if you're interested and willing."

Brendon nodded, then turned to Breck. "Going through this? I found the love of my life, Breck, in Imly. Finding out what happened to her? That changed my focus. I love my woodworking, love working with my hands, but this? This has my heart. So tell Barnabas, it's a yes. Just let me know where and when I'm heading off to school."

Breck laughed before he moved away. "I will do that, Brendon. God bless you, my friend."

Six months later, Brendon searched through the apartment for the lady he still called his bride, not finding her. He paused in the hallway, a hand on his head, frowning before he nodded, heading for the balcony off his office. He stood for a moment, watching the love of his life as she sat, curled up on the love seat, a blanket wrapped around her against the cool spring breeze.

Imly looked up, a smile on her face, reaching for his kiss and then snuggling into his arms as he sat beside her, content with her life. She had found the missing part of her heart, when she found him, or rather God had led her to him. She had her parents back in her life. She was saddened that the people who had raised her had been killed by Tyron Wills as a threat against her that she never understood.

"Have a good day, love?" Brendon was content as well. He was deep into his studies at a local university, eager to learn, and more than ready to set up the department the Board was looking at.

"I did. Hagen was around with the twin. They are so cute. Tiny, but cute. She says Brandon spoils them, but she's content with that. She says that they have what they both wanted. She wanted a boy, he wanted a girl."

Brendon grinned. "He's been walking around six feet off the ground since they came. I am happy for them." He grew silent.

"Mom and Dad were by today. They finalized the sale of their home and found one here in town. I think Bruce helped out that way."

"I'm sure he did. He has a wealth of contacts that are always willing to help him out. He doesn't abuse the contacts that he has."

"No, he wouldn't." Imly bit at her lip. "Brendon, where do we go from here? You're deep in your studies. I'm at loose ends."

"I know you are. You need this time, love, just to be you, to learn how to live once more."

"I know I do, but I'm used to being busy. Bruce suggested that I volunteer at the shelter, but I don't want to. It brings back too many memories."

"It would. You're still working for Lawrence, and he is so thankful for you to be there."

"I know, but I'm not sure I want to continue working in an office. What I really want to do? Learn to paint and stain the furniture as you did. I talked to him today. He wasn't surprised and has promised to teach me, but he made me promise that if we have children, I will step back so the babies aren't harmed."

"I agree with him there. When and if that happens, we'll talk about it."

The young couple grew silent, content to be with one another, sure of the other's love for each other, ready to move on to where God was leading. Just where that was, they weren't sure.

Brendon sighed as his phone chimed. He pulled it out, pulling up a text, and then began to laugh.

———

"What's so funny?" Imly reached for his phone, beginning to laugh. "Buckley! He just doesn't stop. No, I don't want to help him in the church office. But what else is he asking?"

"He has asked if you would be willing to give some talks on what you went through, to show how God protected you and led you to be so thankful and praise Him through it all. We'll pray about it. He'll pester you, no doubt, but he will accept it if you say no."

"I should say yes." Imly laughed. "It would serve him right."

Brendon laughed, then reached down to kiss her before snuggling her back against him. They had no plans that evening, content just to sit and watch the setting sun as it sank over the lake.

Thank you for choosing to read the story of Brendon and the love of his life, Imly. What a ride they took us on. I joke that the characters only allow me to be the driver, that they don't share the map or GPS coordinates with me to tell me where the story is going. Each character has their own unique story and character. That's what I love about discovering each one.

Characters have a habit of showing up in the stories. Dave and his Rylee are from a town I named Riverville. Their story is *A Touch of His* Garment. Doug and Darcie's is *The Heart of a* Lion. But I love it as well when beloved characters walk in and out of other stories. The Emma mentioned? She is from Riverville as well, her story and that of her husband, Abe, being *His Protection* from the *His Guardians* series.

When do we praise God? When skies are blue, everything is rosy, and nothing bad is happening? Or do we praise Him in all things? We need to practice the power of praising Him in all situations. As I write this story, the province and country I live in, Ontario, Canada, is in the second wave of the COVID-19 pandemic. It is difficult to praise in this, but I must. He is in control, even though in our humanness we doubt that.

God bless you, my friends.

Ronna